"Do it," she said, pointing to the floor. "The full down-on-bended-knee thing."

"Seriously?" he said, dark brows raised.

"Yes," she said imperiously.

He grinned. "Okay."

The tall, denim-clad hunk obediently knelt down on one knee, took her right hand in both of his and looked up into her face. "Andie, will you do me the honour of becoming my fake fiancée?" he intoned in that deep, so-sexy voice.

Looking down at his roughly handsome face, Andie didn't know whether to laugh or cry. "Yes, I accept your proposal," she said in a voice that wasn't quite steady.

Dominic squeezed her hand hard as relief flooded his face. He got up from bended knee and, for a moment, she thought he might kiss her.

Dear Reader,

When it comes to Christmas, you'll never hear me say "bah humbug." I love the festive season with all its anticipation, joy and celebrations with family and friends. Each year, I revel in all the baking and decorating and filling the house with Christmas music. We usually have a party on Christmas Eve, lunch with family on the actual day, and then collapse in a heap the next day.

With my love of all things Christmas, you can imagine how much I enjoyed writing *Gift-Wrapped in Her Wedding Dress*, my sixth book for Harlequin Romance.

It was such fun to bring together a billionaire Scrooge who hates Christmas (he's very much a "bah humbug" man!) and a vivacious party planner who loves everything about the season. Dominic Hunt has tragedy and secrets in his past. When he's forced to host a Christmas party for business purposes, lovely Andie Newman breezes into his life and his damaged heart starts to yearn for something more. But Andie has to overcome the pain of past loss before she can open her heart to Dominic—and Dominic has to learn to trust her. I so enjoyed helping these two realize the best Christmas present they could give each other was their love.

In my past life as a magazine editor, I edited magazines with December issues that were totally devoted to Christmas. I've given Andie a magazine background that helps her organize a magnificent party for Dominic that helps them reach out to each other and find their happy-ever-after. Dominic then has some party planning of his own up his sleeve...

I hope you enjoy reading Andie and Dominic's story as much as I enjoyed writing it—and I wish you a Happy Christmas and all the very best for the festive season.

Warm regards,

Kandy

Gift-Wrapped in Her Wedding Dress

Kandy Shepherd

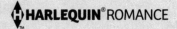

Recycling programs
for this product may
not exist in your area.

ISBN-13: 978-0-373-74362-9

Gift-Wrapped in Her Wedding Dress

First North American Publication 2015

Copyright © 2015 by Kandy Shepherd

Printed in U.S.A.

Kandy Shepherd swapped a career as a magazine editor for a life writing romance. She lives on a small farm in the Blue Mountains near Sydney, Australia, with her husband, daughter and lots of pets. She believes in love at first sight and real-life romance—they worked for her! Kandy loves to hear from her readers. Visit her at kandyshepherd.com.

Books by Kandy Shepherd

Harlequin Romance

The Summer They Never Forgot
The Tycoon and the Wedding Planner
A Diamond in Her Stocking
From Paradise...to Pregnant!
Hired by the Brooding Billionaire

Visit the Author Profile page
at Harlequin.com for more titles.

To all my Christmas magazine colleagues,
in particular Helen, Adriana and Jane—
the magic of the season lives on!

CHAPTER ONE

SO HE'D GOT on the wrong side of the media. Again. Dominic's words, twisted out of all recognition, were all over newspapers, television and social media.

Billionaire businessman Dominic Hunt refuses to sleep out with other CEOs in charity event for homeless.

Dominic slammed his fist on his desk so hard the pain juddered all the way up his arm. He hadn't *refused* to support the charity in their Christmas appeal, just refused the invitation to publicly bed down for the night in a cardboard box on the forecourt of the Sydney Opera House. His donation to the worthy cause had been significant—but anonymous. *Why wasn't that enough?*

He buried his head in his hands. For a harrowing time in his life there had been no choice for him but to sleep rough for real, a cardboard box his only bed. He couldn't go there again—not even for a charity stunt, no matter how worthy. There could be no explanation—he would not share the secrets of his past. *Ever.*

With a sick feeling of dread he continued to read onscreen the highlights of the recent flurry of negative press about him and his company, thoughtfully compiled in a report by his Director of Marketing.

Predictably, the reporters had then gone on to re-hash his well-known aversion to Christmas. Again he'd been misquoted. It was true he loathed the whole idea of celebrating Christmas. But not for the reasons the media had so fancifully contrived. Not because he was a *Scrooge.* How he hated that label and the erroneous aspersions that he didn't ever give to charity. Despaired that he was included in a round-up of Australia's Multi-Million-Dollar Misers. *It couldn't be further from the truth.*

He strongly believed that giving money to worthy causes should be conducted in private—not for public acclaim. But this time he couldn't ignore the name-calling and innuendo. He was near to closing a game-changing deal on a joint venture with a family-owned American corporation run by a man with a strict moral code that included obvious displays of philanthropy.

Dominic could not be seen to be a Scrooge. He had to publicly prove that he was not a miser. But he did not want to reveal the extent of his charitable support because to do so would blow away the smokescreen he had carefully constructed over his past.

He'd been in a bind. Until his marketing director had suggested he would attract positive press if he opened his harbourside home for a lavish fund-raising event for charity. 'Get your name in the newspaper for the right reasons,' he had been advised.

Dominic hated the idea of his privacy being invaded but he had reluctantly agreed. He wanted the joint venture to happen. If a party was what it took, he was prepared to put his qualms aside and commit to it.

The party would be too big an event for it to be organised in-house. His marketing people had got outside companies involved. Trouble was the three so-called 'party planners' he'd been sent so far had been incompetent and he'd shown them the door within minutes of meeting. Now there was a fourth. He glanced down at the eye-catching card on the desk in front of him. Andrea Newman from a company called Party Queens—*No party too big or too small* the card boasted.

Party Queens. It was an interesting choice for a business name. Not nearly as stitched up as the other companies that had pitched for this business. But did it have the gravitas required? After all, this event could be the deciding factor in a deal that would extend his business interests internationally.

He glanced at his watch. This morning he was working from his home office. Ms Newman was due to meet with him right now, here at his house where the party was to take place. Despite the attention-grabbing name of the business, he had no reason to expect Party Planner Number Four to be any more impressive than the other three he'd sent packing. But he would give her twenty minutes—that was only fair and he made a point of always being fair.

On cue, the doorbell rang. Punctuality, at least, was a point in Andrea Newman's favour. He headed down the wide marble stairs to the front door.

His first impression of the woman who stood on his porch was that she was attractive, not in a conventionally pretty way but something rather more interesting—an angular face framed by a tangle of streaked blonde hair, a wide generous mouth, unusual green eyes. So attractive he found himself looking at her for a moment longer than was required to sum up a possible contractor. And the almost imperceptible curve of her mouth let him know she'd noticed.

'Good morning, Mr Hunt—Andie Newman from Party Queens,' she said. 'Thank you for the pass code that got me through the gate. Your se-

curity is formidable, like an eastern suburbs fortress.' Was that a hint of challenge underscoring her warm, husky voice? If so, he wasn't going to bite.

'The pass code expires after one use, Ms Newman,' he said, not attempting to hide a note of warning. The three party planners before her were never going to get a new pass code. But none of them had been remotely like her—in looks or manner.

She was tall and wore a boldly patterned skirt of some silky fine fabric that fell below her knees in uneven layers, topped by a snug-fitting rust-coloured jacket and high heeled shoes that laced all the way up her calf. A soft leather satchel was slung casually across her shoulder. She presented as smart but more unconventional than the corporate dark suits and rigid briefcases of the other three—whose ideas had been as pedestrian as their appearances.

'Andie,' she replied and started to say something else about his security system. But, as she did, a sudden gust of balmy spring breeze whipped up her skirt, revealing long slender legs and a tantalising hint of red underwear. Dominic tried to do the gentlemanly thing and look elsewhere—difficult when she was standing so near to him and her legs were so attention-worthy.

'Oh,' she gasped, and fought with the skirt to hold it down, but no sooner did she get the front of the skirt in place, the back whipped upwards and she had to twist around to hold it down. The back view of her legs was equally as impressive as the front. He balled his hands into fists by his sides so he did not give into the temptation to help her with the flyaway fabric.

She flushed high on elegant cheekbones, blonde hair tousled around her face, and laughed a husky, uninhibited laugh as she battled to preserve her modesty. The breeze died down as quickly as it had sprung up and her skirt floated back into place. Still, he noticed she continued to keep it in check with a hand on her thigh.

'That's made a wonderful first impression, hasn't it?' she said, looking up at him with a rueful smile. For a long moment their eyes connected and he was the first to look away. *She was beautiful.*

As she spoke, the breeze gave a final last sigh that ruffled her hair across her face. Dominic wasn't a fanciful man, but it seemed as though the wind was ushering her into his house.

'There are worse ways of making an impression,' he said gruffly. 'I'm interested to see what you follow up with.'

Andie wasn't sure what to reply. She stood at the threshold of Dominic Hunt's multi-million-dollar mansion and knew for the first time in her career she was in serious danger of losing the professional cool in which she took such pride.

Not because of the incident with the wind and her skirt. Or because she was awestruck by the magnificence of the house and the postcard-worthy panorama of Sydney Harbour that stretched out in front of it. No. It was the man who towered above her who was making her feel so inordinately flustered. Too tongue-tied to come back with a quick quip or clever retort.

'Th…thank you,' she managed to stutter as she pushed the breeze-swept hair back from across her face.

During her career as a stylist for both magazines and advertising agencies, and now as a party planner, she had acquired the reputation of being able to manage difficult people. Which was why her two partners in their fledgling business had voted for her to be the one to deal with Dominic Hunt. Party Queens desperately needed a high-profile booking like this to help them get established. Winning it was now on her shoulders.

She had come to his mansion forewarned that he could be a demanding client. The gossip was that he had been scathing to three other planners from other companies much bigger than theirs before giving them the boot. Then there was his wider reputation as a Scrooge—a man who did not share his multitude of money with others less fortunate. He was everything she did not admire in a person.

Despite that, she been blithely confident Dominic Hunt wouldn't be more than she could handle. Until he had answered that door. Her reaction to him had her stupefied.

She had seen the photos, watched the interviews of the billionaire businessman, had recognised he was good-looking in a dark, brooding way. But no amount of research had prepared her for the pulse-raising reality of this man—tall, broad-shouldered, powerful muscles apparent even in his sleek tailored grey suit. He wasn't pretty-boy handsome. Not with that strong jaw, the crooked nose that looked as though it had been broken by a viciously aimed punch, the full, sensual mouth with the faded white scar on the corner, the spiky black hair. And then there was the almost palpable emanation of power.

She had to call on every bit of her professional savvy to ignore the warm flush that rose up her neck and onto her cheeks, the way her heart thudded into unwilling awareness of Dominic Hunt, not as a client but as a man.

She could not allow that to happen. This job was too important to her and her friends in their new business. *Anyway, dark and brooding wasn't her type.* Her ideal man was sensitive and sunny-natured, like her first lost love, for whom she felt she would always grieve.

She extended her hand, willing it to stay steady,

and forced a smile. 'Mr Hunt, let's start again. Andie Newman from Party Queens.'

His grip in return was firm and warm and he nodded acknowledgement of her greeting. If a mere handshake could send shivers of awareness through her, she could be in trouble here.

Keep it businesslike. She took a deep breath, tilted back her head to meet his gaze full-on. 'I believe I'm the fourth party planner you've seen and I don't want there to be a fifth. I should be the person to plan your event.'

If he was surprised at her boldness, it didn't show in his scrutiny; his grey eyes remained cool and assessing.

'You'd better come inside and convince me why that should be the case,' he said. Even his voice was attractive—deep and measured and utterly masculine.

'I welcome the opportunity,' she said in the most confident voice she could muster.

She followed him into the entrance hall of the restored nineteen-twenties house, all dark stained wood floors and cream marble. A grand central marble staircase with wrought-iron balustrades split into two sides to climb to the next floor. This wasn't the first grand home she'd been in during the course of her work but it was so impressive she had to suppress an impulse to gawk.

'Wow,' she said, looking around her, forgetting

all about how disconcerted Dominic Hunt made her feel. 'The staircase. It's amazing. I can just see a choir there, with a chorister on each step greeting your guests with Christmas carols as they step into the house.' Her thoughts raced ahead of her. Choristers' robes in red and white? Each chorister holding a scrolled parchment printed with the words to the carol? What about the music? A string quartet? A harpsichord?

'What do you mean?' he said, breaking into her reverie.

Andie blinked to bring herself back to earth and turned to look up at him. She smiled. 'Sorry. I'm getting ahead of myself. It was just an idea. Of course I realise I still need to convince you I'm the right person for your job.'

'I meant about the Christmas carols.'

So he would be that kind of pernickety client, pressing her for details before they'd even decided on the bigger picture. Did she need to spell out the message of 'Deck the Halls with Boughs of Holly'?

She shook her head in a don't-worry-about-it way. 'It was just a top-of-mind thought. But a choir would be an amazing use of the staircase. Maybe a children's choir. Get your guests into the Christmas spirit straight away, without being too cheesy about it.'

'It isn't going to be a Christmas party.' He virtually spat the word *Christmas*.

'But a party in December? I thought—'

He frowned and she could see where his reputation came from as his thick brows drew together and his eyes darkened. 'Truth be told, I don't want a party here at all. But it's a necessary evil—necessary to my business, that is.'

'Really?' she said, struggling not to jump in and say the wrong thing. A client who didn't actually want a party? This she hadn't anticipated. Her certainty that she knew how to handle this situation—this man—started to seep away.

She gritted her teeth, forced her voice to sound as conciliatory as possible. 'I understood from your brief that you wanted a big event benefiting a charity in the weeks leading up to Christmas on a date that will give you maximum publicity.'

'All that,' he said. 'Except it's not to be a Christmas party. Just a party that happens to be held around that time.'

Difficult and demanding didn't begin to describe this. But had she been guilty of assuming December translated into Christmas? Had it actually stated that in the brief? She didn't think she'd misread it.

She drew in a calming breath. 'There seems to have been a misunderstanding and I apologise for that,' she said. 'I have the official briefing from your marketing department here.' She patted her satchel. 'But I'd rather hear your thoughts, your ideas for the event in your own words. A success-ful party plan comes from the heart. Can we sit down and discuss this?'

He looked pointedly at his watch. Her heart sank to the level of the first lacing on her shoes. She did not want to be the fourth party planner he fired before she'd even started her pitch. 'I'll give you ten minutes,' he said.

He led her into a living room that ran across the entire front of the house and looked out to the blue waters of the harbour and its icons of the Sydney Harbour Bridge and the Opera House. Glass doors opened out to a large terrace. *A perfect summer party terrace.*

Immediately she recognised the work of one of Sydney's most fashionable high-end interior designers—a guy who only worked with budgets that started with six zeros after them. The room worked neutral tones and metallics in a nod to the art deco era of the original house. The result was masculine but very, very stylish.

What an awesome space for a party. But she forced thoughts of the party out of her head. She had ten minutes to win this business. Ten min-utes to convince Dominic Hunt she was the one he needed.

CHAPTER TWO

DOMINIC SAT ANDIE NEWMAN down on the higher of the two sofas that faced each other over the marble coffee table—the sofa he usually chose to give himself the advantage. He had no need to impress her with his greater height and bulk—she was tall, but he was so much taller than her even as he sat on the lower seat. Besides, the way she positioned herself with shoulders back and spine straight made him think she wouldn't let herself be intimidated by him or by anyone else. *Think again.* The way she crossed and uncrossed those long legs revealed she was more nervous than she cared to let on.

He leaned back in his sofa, pulled out her business card from the inside breast pocket of his suit jacket and held it between finger and thumb. 'Tell me about Party Queens. This seems like a very new, shiny card.'

'Brand new. We've only been in business for three months.'

'We?'

'My two business partners, Eliza Dunne and Gemma Harper. We all worked on a magazine together before we started our own business.'

He narrowed his eyes. 'Now you're "party queens"?' He used his fingers to enclose the two words with quote marks. 'I don't see the connection.'

'We always were party queens—even when we were working on the magazine.' He quirked an eyebrow and she paused. He noticed she quirked an eyebrow too, in unconscious imitation of his action. 'Not in that way.' She tried to backtrack, then smiled. 'Well, maybe somewhat in that way. Between us we've certainly done our share of partying. But then you have to actually enjoy a party to organise one; don't you agree?'

'It's not something I've given thought to,' he said. Business-wise, it could be a point either for her or against her.

Parties had never been high on his agenda—even after his money had opened so many doors for him. Whether he'd been sleeping rough in an abandoned building project in the most dangerous part of Brisbane or hobnobbing with decision makers in Sydney, he'd felt he'd never quite fitted in. So he did the minimum socialising required for his business. 'You were a journalist?' he asked, more than a little intrigued by her.

She shook her head. 'My background is in interior design but when a glitch in the economy meant the company I worked for went bust, I ended up as an interiors editor on a lifestyle magazine. I put together shoots for interiors and products and I loved it. Eliza and Gemma worked on the same magazine, Gemma as the food editor and Eliza on the publishing side. Six months ago we were told out of the blue that the magazine was closing and we had all lost our jobs.'

'That must have been a shock,' he said.

When he'd first started selling real estate at the age of eighteen he'd lived in terror he'd lose his job. Underlying all his success was always still that fear—which was why he was so driven to keep his business growing and thriving. Without money, without a home, he could slide back into being Nick Hunt of 'no fixed abode' rather than Dominic Hunt of Vaucluse, one of the most exclusive addresses in Australia.

'It shouldn't have come as a shock,' she said. 'Magazines close all the time in publishing—it's an occupational hazard. But when it actually happened, when *again* one minute I had a job and the next I didn't, it was…soul-destroying.'

'I'm sorry,' he said.

She shrugged. 'I soon picked myself up.'

He narrowed his eyes. 'It's quite a jump from a magazine job to a party planning business.' Her lack of relevant experience could mean Party Planner Number Four would go the way of the other three. He was surprised at how disappointed that made him feel.

'It might seem that way, but hear me out,' she said, a determined glint in her eye. If one of the other planners had said that, he would have looked pointedly at his watch. This one, he was prepared to listen to—he was actually interested in her story.

'We had to clear our desks immediately and were marched out of the offices by security guards. Shell-shocked, we all retired to a café and thought about what we'd do. The magazine's deputy editor asked could we organise her sister's eighteenth birthday party. At first we said no, thinking she was joking. But then we thought about it. A big magazine shoot that involves themes and food and props is quite a production. We'd also sometimes organise magazine functions for advertisers. We realised that between us we knew a heck of a lot about planning parties.'

'As opposed to enjoying them,' he said.

'That's right,' she said with a smile that seemed reminiscent of past parties enjoyed. 'Between the three of us we had so many skills we could utilise.'

'Can you elaborate on that?'

She held up a slender index finger, her nails tipped with orange polish. 'One, I'm the ideas and visuals person—creative, great with themes and props and highly organised with follow-through.' A second finger went up. 'Two, Gemma trained as a chef and is an amazing food person—food is one of the most important aspects of a good party, whether cooking it yourself or knowing which chefs to engage.'

She had a little trouble getting the third finger to stay straight and swapped it to her pinkie. 'Then, three, Eliza has her head completely around finances and contracts and sales and is also quite the wine buff.'

'So you decided to go into business together?' Her entrepreneurial spirit appealed to him.

She shook her head so her large multi-hoop gold earrings clinked. 'Not then. Not yet. We agreed to do the eighteenth party while we looked for other jobs and freelanced for magazines and ad agencies.'

'How did it work out?' He thought about his eighteenth birthday. It had gone totally unmarked by any celebration—except his own jubilation that he was legally an adult and could never now be recalled to the hell his home had become. It had also marked the age he could be tried as an adult if he had skated too close to the law—though by that time his street-fighting days were behind him.

'There were a few glitches, of course, but over-all it was a great success. The girl went to a posh private school and both girls and parents loved the girly shoe theme we organised. One eighteenth led to another and soon we had other parents clamouring for us to do their kids' parties.'

'Is there much money in parties for kids?' He didn't have to ask all these questions but he was curious. Curious about her as much as anything.

Her eyebrows rose. 'You're kidding, right? We're talking wealthy families on the eastern suburbs and north shore. We're talking one-upmanship.' He enjoyed the play of expressions across her face, the way she gesticulated with her hands as she spoke. 'Heck, we've done a four-year-old's party on a budget of thousands.'

'All that money for a four-year-old?' He didn't have anything to do with kids except through his anonymous charity work. Had given up on his dream he would ever have children of his own. In fact, he was totally out of touch with family life.

'You'd better believe it,' she said.

He was warming to Andie Newman—how could any red-blooded male not?—but he wanted to ensure she was experienced enough to make his event work. All eyes would be on it as up until now he'd been notoriously private. If he threw a party, it had better be a good party. Better than good.

'So when did you actually go into business?'

'We were asked to do more and more parties.

Grown-up parties too. Thirtieths and fortieths, even a ninetieth. It snowballed. Yet we still saw it as a stopgap thing although people suggested we make it a full-time business.'

'A very high percentage of small businesses go bust in the first year,' he couldn't help but warn.

She pulled a face that told him she didn't take offence. 'We were very aware of that. Eliza is the profit and loss spreadsheet maven. But then a public relations company I worked freelance for asked us to do corporate parties and product launches. The work was rolling in. We began to think we should make it official and form our own company.'

'A brave move.' He'd made brave moves in his time—and most of them had paid off. He gave her credit for initiative.

She leaned forward towards him. This close he could appreciate how lovely her eyes were. He didn't think he had ever before met anyone with genuine green eyes. 'We've leased premises in the industrial area of Alexandria and we're firing. But I have to be honest with you—we haven't done anything with potentially such a profile as your party. We want it. We need it. And because we want it to so much we'll pull out every stop to make it a success.'

Party Planner Number Four clocked up more credit for her honesty. He tapped the card on the edge of his hand. 'You've got the enthusiasm; do you have the expertise? Can you assure me you can do my job and do it superlatively well?'

Those remarkable green eyes were unblinking. 'Yes. Absolutely. Undoubtedly. There might only be three of us, but between us we have a zillion contacts in Sydney—chefs, decorators, florists, musicians, waiting staff. If we can't do it ourselves we can pull in the right people who can. And none of us is afraid of the hard work a party this size would entail. We would welcome the challenge.'

He realised she was now sitting on the edge of the sofa, her hands clasped together and her foot crossed over her ankle was jiggling. She really did want this job—wanted it badly.

Dominic hadn't got where he was without a fine-tuned instinct for people. Instincts honed first on the streets where trusting the wrong person could have been fatal and then in the cut-throat business of high-end real estate and property development. His antennae were telling him Andie Newman would be able to deliver—and that he would enjoy working with her.

Trouble was, while he thought she might be the right person for the job, he found her very attractive and would like to ask her out. And he couldn't do both. He *never* dated staff or suppliers. He'd made that mistake with his ex-wife—he would not make it again. Hire Andie Newman and he was more than halfway convinced he would get a good party planner. Not hire her and he could ask her on a date. But he needed this event to work—and for that the planning had to be in the best possible hands. He was torn.

'I like your enthusiasm,' he said. 'But I'd be taking a risk by working with a company that is in many ways still…unproven.'

Her voice rose marginally—she probably didn't notice but to him it betrayed her anxiety to impress. 'We have a file overflowing with references from happy clients. But before you come to any decisions let's talk about what you're expecting from us. The worst thing that can happen is for a client to get an unhappy surprise because we've got the brief wrong.'

She pulled out a folder from her satchel. He liked that it echoed the design of her business card. That showed an attention to detail. The chaos of his early life had made him appreciate planning and order. He recognised his company logo on the printout page she took from the folder and quickly perused.

'So tell me,' she said, when she'd finished reading it. 'I'm puzzled. Despite this briefing document stating the party is to be "A high-profile Christmas event to attract favourable publicity for Dominic Hunt" you still insist it's not to reference Christmas in any way. Which is correct?'

* * *

Andie regretted the words almost as soon as they'd escaped from her mouth. She hadn't meant to confront Dominic Hunt or put him on the spot. Certainly she hadn't wanted to get him offside. But the briefing had been ambiguous and she felt she had to clarify it if she was to secure this job for Party Queens.

She needed their business to succeed—never again did she want to be at the mercy of the whims of a corporate employer. To have a job one day and then suddenly not the next day was too traumatising after that huge personal change of direction she'd had forced upon her five years ago. But she could have put her question with more subtlety.

He didn't reply. The silence that hung between them became more uncomfortable by the second. His face tightened with an emotion she couldn't read. Anger? Sorrow? Regret? Whatever it was, the effect was so powerful she had to force herself not to reach over and put her hand on his arm to comfort him, maybe even hug him. And that would be a mistake. Even more of a mistake than her ill-advised question had been.

She cringed that she had somehow prompted the unleashing of thoughts that were so obviously painful for him. Then braced herself to be booted out on to the same scrapheap as the three party planners who had preceded her.

Finally he spoke, as if the words were being dragged out of him. 'The brief was incorrect. Christmas has some…difficult memories attached to it for me. I don't celebrate the season. Please just leave it at that.' For a long moment his gaze held hers and she saw the anguish recede.

Andie realised she had been holding her breath and she let it out with a slow sigh of relief, amazed he hadn't shown her the door.

'Of…of course,' she murmured, almost gagging with gratitude that she was to be given a second chance. And she couldn't deny that she wanted that chance. Not just for the job but—she could not deny it—the opportunity to see more of this undoubtedly interesting man.

There was something deeper here, some private pain, that she did not understand. But it would be bad-mannered prying to ask any further questions.

She didn't know much about his personal life. Just that he was considered a catch—rich, handsome, successful. *Though not her type, of course.* He lived here alone, she understood, in this street in Vaucluse where house prices started in the double digit millions. Wasn't there a bitter divorce in his background—an aggrieved ex-wife, a public battle for ownership of the house? She'd have to look it up. If she were to win this job—and she understood that it was still a big *if*—she needed to get a grasp on how this man ticked.

'Okay, so that's sorted—no Christmas,' she said, aiming to sound briskly efficient without any nod to the anguish she had read at the back of his eyes. 'Now I know what you *don't* want for your party, let's talk about what you *do* want. I'd like to hear in your words what you expect from this party. Then I can give you my ideas based on your thoughts.'

The party proposals she had hoped to discuss had been based on Christmas; she would have to do some rapid thinking.

Dominic Hunt got up from the sofa and started to pace. He was so tall, his shoulders so broad, he dominated even the large, high-ceilinged room. Andie found herself wondering about his obviously once broken nose—who had thrown the first punch? She got up, not to pace alongside him but to be closer to his level. She did not feel intimidated by him but she could see how he could be intimidating.

'The other planners babbled on about how important it was to invite A-list and B-list celebrities to get publicity. I don't give a damn about celebrities and I can't see how that's the right kind of publicity.'

Andie paused, not sure what to say, only knowing she had to be careful not to *babble on*. 'I can organise the party, but the guest list is up to you and your people.'

He stopped his pacing, stepped closer. 'But do you agree with me?'

Was this a test question? Answer incorrectly and that scrapheap beckoned? As always, she could only be honest. 'I do agree with you. It's my understanding that this party is aimed at...at image repair.'

'You mean repair to my image as a miserly Scrooge who hoards all his money for himself?'

She swallowed a gasp at the bitterness of his words, then looked up at him to see not the anger she expected but a kind of manly bewilderment that surprised her.

'I mightn't have put it quite like that, but yes," she said. 'You do have that reputation and I understand you want to demonstrate it's not so. And yes, I think the presence of a whole lot of free-loading so-called celebrities who run the gamut from the A to the Z list and have nothing to do with the charities you want to be seen to be supporting might not help. But you *are* more likely to get coverage in the social pages if they attend.'

He frowned. 'Is there such a thing as a Z-list celebrity?'

She laughed. 'If there isn't, there should be. Maybe I made it up.'

'You did say you were creative,' he said. He smiled—the first real smile she'd seen from him. It transformed his face, like the sun coming out from behind a dark storm cloud, unleashing an unexpected charm. Her heartbeat tripped into double time like it had the first moment she'd seen him. Why? Why this inexplicable reaction to a man she should dislike for his meanness and greed?

She made a show of looking around her to disguise her consternation. Tamed the sudden shakiness in her voice into a businesslike tone. 'How many magazines or lifestyle programmes have featured this house?' she asked.

'None. They never will,' he said.

'Good,' she said. 'The house is both magnificent and unknown. I reckon even your neighbours would be willing to cough up a sizeable donation just to see inside.' In her mind's eye she could see the house transformed into a glittering party paradise. 'The era of the house is nineteen-twenties, right?'

'Yes,' he said. 'It was originally built for a wealthy wool merchant.'

She thought some more. 'Why not an extravagant *Great Gatsby* twenties-style party with a silver and white theme—that gives a nod to the festive season—and a strictly curated guest list? Guests would have to dress in silver or white. Or both. Make it very exclusive, an invitation to be sought after. The phones of Sydney's social set would be set humming to see who got one or not.'

Her eyes half shut as her mind bombarded her with images. 'Maybe a masked party. Yes. Amazing silver and white masks. Bejewelled and befeathered. Fabulous masks that could be auctioned off at some stage for your chosen charity.'

'Auctioned?'

Her eyes flew open and she had to orientate herself back into the reality of the empty room that she had just been envisioning filled with elegant partygoers. Sometimes when her creativity was firing she felt almost in a trance. Then it was her turn to frown. How could a Sydney billionaire be such a party innocent?

Even she, who didn't move in the circles of society that attended lavish fund-raising functions, knew about the auctions. The competitive bidding could probably be seen as the same kind of one-upmanship as the spending of thousands on a toddler's party. 'I believe it's usual to have a fund-raising auction at these occasions. Not just the masks, of course. Other donated items. Something really big to up the amount of dollars for your charity.' She paused. 'You're a property developer, aren't you?'

He nodded. 'Among other interests.'

'Maybe you could donate an apartment? There'd be some frenzied bidding for that from people hoping for a bargain. And you would look generous.'

His mouth turned down in an expression of distaste. 'I'm not sure that's in keeping with the image I want to…to reinvent.'

Privately she agreed with him—why couldn't people just donate without expecting a lavish party in return? But she kept her views to herself. Creating those lavish parties was her job now.

'That's up to you and your people. The guest list and the auction, I mean. But the party? That's my domain. Do you like the idea of the twenties theme to suit the house?' In her heart she still longed for the choristers on the staircase. Maybe it would have to be a jazz band on the steps. That could work. Not quite the same romanticism and spirit as Christmas, but it would be a spectacular way to greet guests.

'I like it,' he said slowly.

She forced herself not to panic, not to bombard him with a multitude of alternatives. 'If not that idea, I have lots of others. I would welcome the opportunity to present them to you.'

He glanced at his watch and she realised she had been there for much longer than the ten-minute pitch he'd allowed. Surely that was a good sign.

'I'll schedule in another meeting with you tomorrow afternoon,' he said.

'You mean a second interview?' she asked, fingers crossed behind her back.

'No. A brainstorming session. You've got the job, Ms Newman.'

It was only as, jubilant, she made her way to the door—conscious of his eyes on her back—that she wondered at the presence of a note of regret in Dominic Hunt's voice.

CHAPTER THREE

TRY AS SHE MIGHT, Andie couldn't get excited about the nineteen-twenties theme she had envisaged for Dominic Hunt's party. It would be lavish and glamorous and she would enjoy every moment of planning such a visually splendid event. Such a party would be a spangled feather in Party Queens' cap. But it seemed somehow *wrong*.

The feeling niggled at her. How could something so extravagant, so limited to those who could afford the substantial donation that would be the cost of entrance make Dominic Hunt look less miserly? Even if he offered an apartment for auction—and there was no such thing as a cheap apartment in Sydney—and raised a lot of money, wouldn't it be a wealthy person who benefited? Might he appear to be a Scrooge hanging out with other rich people who might or might not also be Scrooges? Somehow, it reeked of...well, there was no other word but hypocrisy.

It wasn't her place to be critical—the media-

attention-grabbing party was his marketing people's idea. Her job was to plan the party and make
it as memorable and spectacular as possible. But
she resolved to bring up her reservations in the
brainstorming meeting with him. *If she dared.*

She knew it would be a fine line to tread—
she did not want to risk losing the job for Party
Queens—but she felt she had to give her opinion.
After that she would just keep her mouth shut and
concentrate on making his event the most memorable on the December social calendar.

She dressed with care for the meeting, which
was again at his Vaucluse mansion. *An outfit that
posed no danger of showing off her underwear.*
Slim white trousers, a white top, a string of outsize turquoise beads, silver sandals that strapped
around her ankles. At the magazine she'd made
friends with the fashion editor and still had access to sample sales and special deals. She felt her
wardrobe could hold its own in whatever company
she found herself in—even on millionaire row.

'I didn't risk wearing that skirt,' she blurted out
to Dominic Hunt as he let her into the house. 'Even
though there doesn't appear to be any wind about.'

Mentally she slammed her hand against her
forehead. What a dumb top-of-mind remark to
make to a client. But he still made her nervous. Try
as she might, she couldn't shake that ever-present
awareness of how attractive he was.

His eyes flickered momentarily to her legs. 'Shame,' he said in that deep, testosterone-edged voice that thrilled through her.

Was he flirting with her?

'It...it was a lovely skirt,' she said. 'Just...just rather badly behaved.' How much had he seen when her skirt had flown up over her thighs?

'I liked it very much,' he said.

'The prettiness of its fabric or my skirt's bad behaviour?'

She held his cool grey gaze for a second longer than she should.

'Both,' he said.

She took a deep breath and tilted her chin upward. 'I'll take that as a compliment,' she said with a smile she hoped radiated aplomb. 'Thank you, Mr Hunt.'

'Dominic,' he said.

'Dominic,' she repeated, liking the sound of his name on her lips. 'And thank you again for this opportunity to plan your party.' *Bring it back to business.*

In truth, she would have liked to tell him how good he looked in his superbly tailored dark suit and dark shirt but she knew her voice would come out all choked up. Because it wasn't the Italian elegance of his suit that she found herself admiring. It was the powerful, perfectly proportioned male body that inhabited it. And she didn't want to reveal even a hint of that. *He was a client.*

He nodded in acknowledgement of her words. 'Come through to the back,' he said. 'You can see how the rooms might work for the party.'

She followed him through where the grand staircase split—a choir really would be amazing ranged on the steps—over pristine marble floors to a high-ceilinged room so large their footsteps echoed as they walked into the centre of it. Furnished minimally in shades of white, it looked ready for a high-end photo shoot. Arched windows and a wall of folding doors opened through to an elegant art deco style swimming pool and then to a formal garden planted with palm trees and rows of budding blue agapanthus.

For a long moment Andie simply absorbed the splendour of the room. 'What a magnificent space,' she said finally. 'Was it originally a ballroom?'

'Yes. Apparently the wool merchant liked to entertain in grand style. But it wasn't suited for modern living, which is why I opened it up through to the terrace when I remodelled the house.'

'You did an awesome job,' she said. In her mind's eye she could see flappers in glittering dresses trimmed with feathers and fringing, and men in dapper suits doing the Charleston. Then had to blink, not sure if she was imagining what the room had once been or how she'd like it to be for Dominic's party.

'The people who work for me did an excellent job,' he said.

'As an interior designer I give them full marks,' she said. She had gone to university with Dominic's designer. She just might get in touch with him, seeking inside gossip into what made Dominic Hunt tick.

She looked around her. 'Where's the kitchen? Gemma will shoot me if I go back without reporting to her on the cooking facilities.'

'Through here.'

Andie followed him through to an adjoining vast state-of-the-art kitchen, gleaming in white marble and stainless steel. The style was sleek and modern but paid homage to the vintage of the house. She breathed out a sigh of relief and pleasure. A kitchen like this would make catering for hundreds of guests so much easier. Not that the food was her department. Gemma kept that under her control. 'It's a superb kitchen. Do you cook?'

Was Dominic the kind of guy who ate out every night and whose refrigerator contained only cartons of beer? Or the kind who excelled at cooking and liked to show off his skills to a breathlessly admiring female audience?

'I can look after myself,' he said shortly. 'That includes cooking.'

That figured. After yesterday's meeting she had done some research into Dominic Hunt—though there wasn't much information dating back further than a few years. Along with his comments about celebrating Christmas being a waste of space, he'd also been quoted as saying he would never marry again. From the media accounts, his marriage in his mid-twenties had been short, tumultuous and public, thanks to his ex-wife's penchant for spilling the details to the gossip columns.

'The kitchen and its position will be perfect for the caterers,' she said. 'Gemma will be delighted.'

'Good,' he said.

'You must love this house.' She could not help a wistful note from edging her voice. As an interior designer she knew only too well how much the remodelling would have cost. Never in a million years would she live in a house like this. He was only a few years older than her—thirty-two to her twenty-eight—yet it was as if they came from different planets.

He shrugged those impressively broad shoulders. 'It's a spectacular house. But it's just a house. I never get attached to places.'

Or people?

Her online research had showed him snapped by paparazzi with a number of long-legged beauties—but no woman more than once or twice. *What did it matter to her?*

She patted her satchel. *Back to business.* 'I've come prepared for brainstorming,' she said. 'Have you had any thoughts about the nineteen-twenties theme I suggested?'

'I've thought,' he said. He paused. 'I've thought about it a lot.'

His tone of voice didn't give her cause for confidence. 'You...like it? You don't like it? Because if you don't I have lots of other ideas that would work as well. I—'

He put up his right hand to halt her—large, well sculpted, with knuckles that looked as if they'd sustained scrapes over the years. His well-spoken accent and obvious wealth suggested injuries sustained from boxing or rugby at a private school; the tightly leashed power in those muscles, that strong jaw, gave thought to injuries sustained in something perhaps more visceral.

'It's a wonderful idea for a party,' he said. 'Perfect for this house. Kudos to you, Ms Party Queen.'

'Thank you.' She made a mock curtsy and was pleased when he smiled. *How handsome he was without that scowl.* 'However, is that a "but" I hear coming on?'

He pivoted on his heel so he faced out to the pool, gleaming blue and pristine in the afternoon sun of a late-spring day in mid-November. His back view was impressive, broad shoulders tapering to a tight, muscular rear end. Then he turned back to face her. 'It's more than one "but",' he said. 'The party, the guest list, the—'

'The pointlessness of it all?' she ventured.

He furrowed his brow. 'What makes you say that?'

She found herself twisting the turquoise beads on her necklace between her finger and thumb. Her business partners would be furious with her if she lost Party Queens this high-profile job because she said what she *wanted* to say rather than what she *should* say.

'This party is all about improving your image, right? To make a statement that you're not the... the Scrooge people think you are.'

The fierce scowl was back. 'I'd rather you didn't use the word Scrooge.'

'Okay,' she said immediately. But she would find it difficult to stop *thinking* it. 'I'll try again: that you're not a...a person lacking in the spirit of giving.'

'That doesn't sound much better.' She couldn't have imagined his scowl could have got any darker but it did. 'The party is meant to be a public display of something I would rather be kept private.'

'So...you give privately to charity?'

'Of course I do but it's not your or anyone else's business.'

Personally, she would be glad if he wasn't as tight-fisted as his reputation decreed. But this was about more than what she felt. She could not back down. 'If that's how you feel, tell me again why you're doing this.'

He paused. 'If I share with you the reason why I agreed to holding this party, it's not to leave this room.'

'Of course,' she said. A party planner had to be discreet. It was astounding what family secrets got aired in the planning of a party. She leaned closer, close enough to notice that he must be a twice-a-day-shave guy. *Lots of testosterone, all right.*

'I've got a big joint venture in the United States on the point of being signed. My potential business partner, Walter Burton, is the head of a family company and he is committed to public displays of philanthropy. It would go better with me if I was seen to be the same.'

Andie made a motion with her fingers of zipping her lips shut. 'I... I understand,' she said. Disappointment shafted through her. *So he really was a Scrooge.*

She'd found herself wanting Dominic to be someone better than he was reputed to be. But the party, while purporting to be a charity event, was simply a smart business ploy. More about greed than good-heartedness.

'Now you can see why it's so important,' he said.

Should she say what she thought? The scrapheap of discarded party planners beckoned again. She could imagine her silver-sandal-clad foot kicking feebly from the top of it and hoped it would be a soft landing.

She took a deep steadying breath. 'Cynical journalists might have a field-day with the hypocrisy of a Scrooge—*sorry!*—trying to turn over a new gilded leaf in such an obvious and staged way.'

To her surprise, something like relief relaxed the tense lines of his face. 'That's what I thought too.'

'You...you did?'

'I could see the whole thing backfiring and me no better off in terms of reputation. Possibly worse.'

If she didn't stop twisting her necklace it would break and scatter her beads all over the marble floor. 'So—help me out here. We're back to you not wanting a party?'

She'd talked him out of the big, glitzy event Party Queens really needed. Andie cringed at the prospect of the combined wrath of Gemma and Eliza when she went back to their headquarters with the contract that was sitting in her satchel waiting for his signature still unsigned.

'You know I don't.' *Thank heaven.* 'But maybe a different kind of event,' he said.

'Like...handing over a giant facsimile cheque to a charity?' Which would be doing her right out of a job.

'Where's the good PR in that?'

'In fact it could look even more cynical than the party.'

'Correct.'

He paced a few long strides away from her and then back. 'I'm good at turning one dollar into lots of dollars. That's my skill. Not planning parties. But surely I can get the kind of publicity my marketing department wants, impress my prospective business partner and actually help some less advantaged people along the way?'

She resisted the urge to high-five him. 'To tell you the truth, I couldn't sleep last night for thinking that exact same thing.' *Was it wise to have admitted that?*

'Me too,' he said. 'I tossed and turned all night.'

A sudden vision of him in a huge billionaire's bed, all tangled in the sheets wearing nothing but…well nothing but a billionaire's birthday suit, flashed through her mind and sizzled through her body. *Not my type. Not my type.* She had to repeat it like a mantra.

She willed her heartbeat to slow and hoped he took the flush on her cheekbones for enthusiasm. 'So we're singing from the same hymn sheet. Did you have any thoughts on solving your dilemma?'

'That's where you come in; you're the party expert.'

She hesitated. 'During my sleepless night, I did think of something. But you might not like it.'

'Try me,' he said, eyes narrowed.

'It's out of the ball park,' she warned.

'I'm all for that,' he said.

She flung up her hands in front of her face to act as a shield. 'It...it involves Christmas.'

He blanched under the smooth olive of his tan. 'I told you—'

His mouth set in a grim line, his hands balled into fists by his sides. Should she leave well enough alone? After all, he had said the festive season had difficult associations for him. 'What is it that you hate so much about Christmas?' she asked. She'd always been one to dive straight into the deep end.

'I don't *hate* Christmas.' He cursed under his breath. 'I'm misquoted once and the media repeat it over and over.'

'But—'

He put up his hand to halt her. 'I don't have to justify anything to you. But let me give you three good reasons why I don't choose to celebrate Christmas and all the razzmatazz that goes with it.'

'Fire away,' she said, thinking it wasn't appropriate for her to counter with three things she adored about the festive season. This wasn't a debate. It was a business brainstorming.

'First—the weather is all wrong,' he said. 'It's

hot when it should be cold. A *proper* Christmas is a northern hemisphere Christmas—snow, not sand.'

Not true, she thought. For a born-and-bred Australian like her, Christmas was all about the long, hot sticky days of summer. Cicadas chirruping in the warm air as the family walked to a midnight church service. Lunch outdoors, preferably around a pool or at the beach. Then it struck her—Dominic had a distinct trace of an English accent. That might explain his aversion to festivities Down Under style. But something still didn't seem quite right. His words sounded…too practised, as if he'd recited them a hundred times before.

He continued, warming to his point as she wondered about the subtext to his spiel. 'Then there's the fact that the whole thing is over-commercialised to the point of being ludicrous. I saw Christmas stuff festooning the shops in September.'

She almost expected him to snarl a Scrooge-like *Bah! Humbug!* but he obviously restrained himself.

'You have a point,' she said. 'And carols piped through shopping malls in October? So annoying.'

'Quite right,' he said. 'This whole obsession with extended Christmas celebrations, it…it… makes people who don't celebrate it—for one reason or another—feel…feel excluded.'

His words faltered and he looked away in the direction of the pool but not before she'd seen the bleakness in his eyes. She realised those last words hadn't been rehearsed. That he might be regretting them. Again she had that inane urge to comfort him—without knowing why he needed comforting.

She knew she had to take this carefully. 'Yes,' she said slowly. 'I know what you mean.' That first Christmas without Anthony had been the bleakest imaginable. And each year after she had thought about him and the emptiness in her heart he had left behind him. But she would not share that with this man; it was far too personal. And nothing to do with the general discussion about Christmas.

His mouth twisted. 'Do you?'

She forced her voice to sound cheerful and impersonal. Her ongoing sadness over Anthony was deeply private. 'Not me personally. I love Christmas. I'm lucky enough to come from a big family—one of five kids. I have two older brothers and a sister and a younger sister. Christmas with our extended family was always—still is—a special time of the year. But my parents knew that wasn't the case for everyone. Every year we shared our celebration with children who weren't as fortunate as we were.'

'Charity cases, you mean,' he said, his voice hard-edged with something she couldn't identify.

'In the truest sense of the word,' she said. 'We didn't query them being there. It meant more kids to play with on Christmas Day. It didn't even enter our heads that there would be fewer presents for us so they could have presents too. Two of them moved in with us as long-term foster kids. When I say I'm from five, I really mean from seven. Only that's too confusing to explain.'

He gave a sound that seemed a cross between a grunt and a cynical snort.

She shrugged, inexplicably hurt by his reaction. 'You might think it goody-two-shoes-ish but that's the way my family are, and I love them for it,' she said, her voice stiff and more than a touch defensive.

'Not at all,' he said. 'I think it…it sounds wonderful. You were very lucky to grow up in a family like that.' With the implication being he hadn't?

'I know, and I'm thankful. And my parents' strong sense of community didn't do us any harm. In fact those Christmas Days my family shared with others got me thinking. It was what kept me up last night. I had an idea.'

'Fire away,' he said.

She channelled all her optimism and enthusiasm to make her voice sound convincing to Sydney's most notorious Scrooge. 'Wouldn't it be wonderful if you opened this beautiful home on Christmas Day for a big lunch party for children and families who do it hard on Christmas Day? Not as a gimmick. Not as a stunt. As a genuine act of hospitality and sharing the true spirit of Christmas.'

CHAPTER FOUR

DOMINIC STARED AT Andie in disbelief. Hadn't she heard a word he'd said about his views on Christmas? She looked up at him, her eyes bright with enthusiasm but backlit by wariness. 'Please, just consider my proposal,' she said. 'That's all I ask.' He could easily fire her for straying so far from the brief and she must know it—yet that didn't stop her. Her tenacity was to be admired.

Maybe she had a point. No matter what she or anyone else thought, he was not a Scrooge or a hypocrite. To make a holiday that could never be happy for him happy for others had genuine appeal. He was aware Christmas *was* a special time for a huge percentage of the population. It was just too painful for him to want to do anything but lock himself away with a bottle of bourbon from Christmas Eve to Boxing Day.

Deep from within, he dredged memories of his first Christmas away from home. Aged seventeen, he'd been living in an underground car park beneath an abandoned shopping centre project. His companions had been a ragtag collection of other runaways, addicts, criminals and people who'd lost all hope of a better life. Someone had stolen a branch of a pine tree from somewhere and decorated it with scavenged scraps of glittery paper. They'd all stood around it and sung carols with varying degrees of sobriety. Only he had stood aloof.

Now, he reached out to where Andie was twisting her necklace so tightly it was in danger of snapping. Gently, he disengaged her hand and freed the string of beads. Fought the temptation to hold her hand for any longer than was necessary—slender and warm in his own much bigger hand. Today her nails were painted turquoise. And, as he'd noticed the day before, her fingers were free of any rings.

'Your idea could have merit,' he said, stepping back from her. Back from her beautiful interesting face, her intelligent eyes, the subtle spicy-sweet scent of her. 'Come and sit outside by the pool and we can talk it over.'

Her face flushed with relief at his response and he realised again what spunk it had taken for her to propose something so radical. He was grateful to whoever had sent Party Planner Number Four his way. Andie was gorgeous, smart and not the slightest in awe of him and his money, which was refreshing. His only regret was that he could not both employ her and date her.

He hadn't told the complete truth about why he'd been unable to sleep the night before. Thoughts of her had been churning through his head as much as concerns about the party. He had never felt so instantly attracted to a woman. Ever. If they had met under other circumstances he would have asked her out by now.

'I really think it could work,' she said as she walked with him through the doors and out to the pool area.

For a heart-halting second he thought Andie had tuned into his private thoughts—that she thought dating her could work. *Never.* He'd met his ex-wife, Tara, when she'd worked for his company, with disastrous consequences. The whole marriage had, in fact, been disastrous—based on lies and deception. He wouldn't make that mistake again—even for this intriguing woman.

But of course Andie was talking about her party proposal in businesslike tones. 'You could generate the right kind of publicity—both for your potential business partner and in general,' she said as he settled her into one of the white outdoor armchairs that had cost a small fortune because of its vintage styling.

'While at the same time directly benefiting people who do it tough on the so-called Big Day,' he said as he took the chair next to her.

'Exactly,' she said with her wide, generous smile. When she smiled like that it made him want to make her do it again, just for the pleasure of seeing her face light up. *Not a good idea.*

Her chair was in the shade of one of the mature palm trees he'd had helicoptered in for the landscaping but the sun was dancing off the aqua surface of the pool. He was disappointed when she reached into her satchel, pulled out a pair of tortoiseshell-rimmed sunglasses and donned them against the glare. They looked 'vintage' too. In fact, in her white clothes and turquoise necklace, she looked as if she belonged here.

'In principal, I don't mind your idea,' he said. 'In fact I find it more acceptable than the other.'

Her smile was edged with relief. 'I can't tell you how pleased that makes me.'

'Would the lunch have to be on actual Christmas Day?' he said.

'You could hold it on Christmas Eve or the week leading up to Christmas. In terms of organisation, that would be easier. But none of those peripheral days is as lonely and miserable as Christmas Day can be if you're one…one of the excluded ones,' she said. 'My foster sister told me that.'

The way she was looking at him, even with those too-perceptive green eyes shaded from his view, made him think she was beginning to suspect he had a deeply personal reason for his anti-Christmas stance.

He'd only ever shared that reason with one woman—Melody, the girl who'd first captivated, then shredded, his teenage heart back in that car park squat. By the time Christmas had loomed in the first year of his marriage to Tara, he'd known he'd never be sharing secrets with her. But there was something disarming about Andie that seemed to invite confidences—something he had to stand guard against. She might not be what she seemed—and he had learned the painful lesson not to trust his first impressions when it came to beautiful women.

'I guess any other day doesn't have the same impact,' he reluctantly agreed, not sure he would be able to face the festivities. Did he actually have to be present on the day? Might it not be enough to provide the house and the meal? No. To achieve his goal, he knew his presence would be necessary. Much as he would hate every minute of it.

'Maybe your marketing people will have other ideas,' she said. 'But I think opening your home on the actual December twenty-five to give people who really need it a slap-up feast would be a marvellous antidote to your Scrooge…sorry, *miser*… I mean *cheap* reputation.' She pulled a face. 'Sorry. I didn't actually mean any of those things.'

Why did it sting so much more coming from her? 'Of course you did. So does everyone else. People who have no idea of what and where I might give without wanting any fanfare.' The main reason he wanted to secure the joint venture was to ensure his big project in Brisbane would continue to be funded long after his lifetime.

She looked shamefaced. 'I'm sorry.'

He hated that people like Andie thought he was stingy. Any remaining reservations he might hold about the party had to go. He needed to take action before this unfair reputation become so deeply entrenched he'd never free himself from it. 'Let's hope the seasonal name-calling eases if I go ahead with the lunch.'

She held up a finger in warning. 'It wouldn't appease everyone. Those cynical journalists might not be easily swayed.'

He scowled. 'I can't please everyone.' But he found himself, irrationally, wanting to please *her*.

'It might help if you followed through with a visible, ongoing relationship with a charity. If the media could see…could see…'

Her eyes narrowed in concentration. He waited for the end of her sentence but it wasn't forthcoming. 'See what?'

'Sorry,' she said, shaking her head as if bringing herself back to earth. 'My thoughts tend to run faster than my words sometimes when I'm deep in the creative zone.'

'I get it,' he said, though he wasn't sure what the hell being in the creative zone meant.

'I meant your critics might relent if they could see your gesture was genuine.'

He scowled. 'But it *will* be genuine.'

'You know it and I know it but they might see it as just another publicity gimmick.' Her eyes narrowed again and he gave her time to think. 'What if you didn't actually seek publicity for this day? You know—no invitations or press releases. Let the details leak. Tantalise the media.'

'For a designer, you seem to know a lot about publicity,' he said.

She shrugged. 'When you work in magazines you pick up a lot about both seeking and giving publicity. But your marketing people would have their own ideas, I'm sure.'

'I should talk it over with them,' he said.

'As it's only six weeks until Christmas, and this would be a big event to pull together, may I suggest there's not a lot of discussion time left?'

'You're right. I know. But it's a big deal.' So much bigger for him personally than she realised.

'You're seriously considering going ahead with it?'

He so much preferred it to the Z-list celebrity party. 'Yes. Let's do it.'

She clapped her hands together. 'I'm so glad. We can make it a real dream-come-true for your guests.'

'What about you and your business partners? You'd have to work on Christmas Day.'

'Speaking for me, I'd be fine with working. True spirit of Christmas and all that. I'll have to speak to Gemma and Eliza, but I think they'd be behind it too.' Securing Dominic Hunt's business for Party Queens was too important for them to refuse.

'What about caterers and so on?' he asked.

'The hospitality industry works three hundred and sixty-five days a year. It shouldn't be a problem. There are also people who don't celebrate Christmas as part of their culture who are very happy to work—especially for holiday pay rates. You don't have to worry about all that—that's our job.'

'And the guests? How would we recruit them?' He was about to say he could talk to people in Brisbane, where he was heavily involved in a homeless charity, but stopped himself. That was too connected to the secret part of his life he had no desire to share.

'I know the perfect person to help—my older sister, Hannah, is a social worker. She would know exactly which charities to liaise with. I think she would be excited to be involved.'

It was her. *Andie.* He would not be considering this direction if it wasn't for her. The big glitzy party had seemed so wrong. She made him see what could be right.

'Could we set up a meeting with your sister?' he asked.

'I can do better than that,' she said with a triumphant toss of her head that set her oversized earrings swaying. 'Every Wednesday night is open house dinner at my parents' house. Whoever of my siblings can make it comes. Sometimes grandparents and cousins too. I know Hannah will be there tonight and I'm planning to go too. Why don't you come along?'

'To your family dinner?' His first thought was to say no. Nothing much intimidated him—but meeting people's families was near the top of the list.

'Family is an elastic term for the Newmans. Friends, waifs and strays are always welcome at the table.'

What category would he be placed under? His memory of being a real-life stray made him wince. Friend? Strictly speaking, if circumstances were different, he'd want to be more than friends with Andie. Would connecting with her family create an intimacy he might later come to regret?

He looked down at his watch. Thought about his plan to return to the office.

'We need to get things moving,' she prompted.

'I would like to meet your sister tonight.'

Her wide smile lit her eyes. 'I have a really good feeling about this.'

'Do you always go on your feelings?' he asked.

She took off her sunglasses so he was treated to the directness of her gaze. 'All the time. Don't you?'

If he acted on his feelings he would be insisting they go to dinner, just the two of them. He would be taking her in his arms. Tasting her lovely mouth. Touching. Exploring. *But that wouldn't happen.*

He trusted his instincts when it came to business. But trusting his feelings when it came to women had only led to bitterness, betrayal and the kind of pain he never wanted to expose himself to again.

No to feeling. *Yes* to pleasant relationships that mutually fulfilled desires and were efficiently terminated before emotions ever became part of it. And with none of the complications that came with still having to work with that person. Besides, he suspected the short-term liaison that was all he had to offer would not be acceptable to Andie. She had *for ever* written all over her.

Now it was her turn to look at her watch. 'I'll call my mother to confirm you'll be joining us for dinner. How about I swing by and pick you up at around six?'

He thought about his four o'clock meeting. 'That's early for dinner.'

'Not when there are kids involved.'

'Kids?'

'I have a niece and two nephews. One of the nephews belongs to Hannah. He will almost certainly be there, along with his cousins.'

Dominic wasn't sure exactly what he was letting himself in for. One thing was for certain—he couldn't have seen himself going to a family dinner with any of Party Planners Numbers One to Three. And he suspected he might be in for more than one surprise from gorgeous Party Planner Number Four.

Andie got up from the chair. Smoothed down her white trousers. They were nothing as revealing as her flyaway skirt but made no secret of her slender shape.

'By the way, I'm apologising in advance for my car.'

He frowned. 'Why apologise?'

'I glimpsed your awesome sports car in the garage as I came in yesterday. You might find my hand-me-down hatchback a bit of a comedown.'

He frowned. 'I didn't come into this world behind the wheel of an expensive European sports car. I'm sure your hatchback will be perfectly fine.'

Just how did she see him? His public image— Scrooge, miser, rich guy—was so at odds with the person he knew himself to be. That he wanted her to know. But he could not reveal himself to her without uncovering secrets he would rather leave buried deep in his past.

CHAPTER FIVE

DOMINIC HAD FACED down some fears in his time. But the prospect of being paraded before Andie's large family ranked as one of the most fearsome. As Andie pulled up her hatchback—old but in good condition and nothing to be ashamed of—in front of her parents' home in the northern suburb of Willoughby, sweat prickled on his forehead and his hands felt clammy. How the hell had he got himself into this?

She turned off the engine, took out the keys, unclipped her seat belt and smoothed down the legs of her sleek, very sexy leather trousers. But she made no effort to get out of the car. She turned her head towards him. 'Before we go inside to meet my family I… I need to tell you something first. Something…something about me.'

Why did she look so serious, sombre even? 'Sure, fire away,' he said.

'I've told them you're a client. That there is absolutely nothing personal between us.'

'Of course,' he said.

Strange how at the same time he could be relieved and yet offended by her categorical denial that there ever could be anything *personal* between them.

Now a hint of a smile crept to the corners of her mouth. 'The thing is…they won't believe me. You're good-looking, you're smart and you're personable.'

'That's nice of you to say that,' he said. He noticed she hadn't added that he was rich to his list of attributes.

'You know it's true,' she said. 'My family are determined I should have a man in my life and have become the most inveterate of matchmakers. I expect they'll pounce on you. It could get embarrassing.'

'You're single?' He welcomed the excuse to ask.

'Yes. I… I've been single for a long time. Oh, I date. But I haven't found anyone special since… since…' She twisted right around in the car seat to fully face him. She clasped her hands together on her lap, then started to twist them without seeming to realise she was doing it. 'You need to know this before we go inside.' The hint of a smile had completely dissipated.

'If you think so,' he said. She was twenty-eight and single. What was the big deal here?

'I met Anthony on my first day of university.

We were inseparable from the word go. There was no doubt we would spend our lives together.'

Dominic braced himself for the story of a nasty break-up. Infidelity? Betrayal? A jerk in disguise as a nice guy? He was prepared to make polite noises in response. He knew all about betrayal. But a *quid pro quo* exchange over relationships gone wrong was not something he ever wanted to waste time on with Andie or anyone else.

'It ended?' he said, making a terse contribution only because it was expected.

'He died.'

Two words stated so baldly but with such a wealth of pain behind them. Dominic felt as if he'd been punched in the chest. Nothing he said could be an adequate response. 'Andie, I'm sorry,' was all he could manage.

'It was five years ago. He was twenty-three. He…he went out for an early-morning surf and didn't come back.' He could hear the effort it took for her to keep her tone even.

He knew about people who didn't come back. Goodbyes left unsaid. Personal tragedy. That particular kind of pain. 'Did he…? Did you—?'

'He…he washed up two days later.' She closed her eyes as if against an unbearable image.

'What happened?' He didn't want her to think he was interrogating her on something so sensitive, but he wanted to find out.

'Head injury. An accident. The doctors couldn't be sure exactly how it happened. A rock? His board? A sandbank? We'll never know.'

'Thank you for telling me.' He felt unable to say anything else.

'Better for you to know than not to know when you're about to meet the family. Just in case someone says something that might put you on the spot.'

She heaved a sigh that seemed to signal she had said what she felt she had to say and that there would be no further confidences. Why should there be? *He was just a client.* Something prompted him to want to ask—was she over the loss? Had she moved on? But it was not his place. Client and contractor—that was all they could be to each other. Besides, could anyone *ever* get over loss like that?

'You needed to be in the picture.' She went to open her door. 'Now, let's go in—Hannah is looking forward to meeting you. As I predicted, she's very excited about getting involved.'

Her family's home was a comfortable older-style house set in a chaotic garden in a suburb where values had rocketed in recent years. In the car on the way over, Andie had told him she had lived in this house since she was a baby. All her siblings had. He envied her that certainty, that security.

'Hellooo!' she called ahead of her. 'We're here.'

He followed her down a wide hallway, the walls crammed with framed photographs. They ranged from old-fashioned sepia wedding photos, dating from pre-Second World War, to posed studio shots of cherubic babies. Again he found himself envying her—he had only a handful of family photos to cherish.

At a quick glance he found two of Andie—one in a green checked school uniform with her hair in plaits and that familiar grin showing off a gap in her front teeth; another as a teenager in a flowing pink formal dress. A third caught his eye—an older Andie in a bikini, arm in arm with a tall blond guy in board shorts who was looking down at her with open adoration. The same guy was with her in the next photo, only this time they were playing guitars and singing together. Dominic couldn't bear to do more than glance at them, aware of the tragedy that had followed.

Just before they reached the end of the corridor, Andie stopped and took a step towards him. She stood so close he breathed in her scent—something vaguely oriental, warm and sensual. She leaned up to whisper into his ear and her hair tickled his neck. He had to close his eyes to force himself from reacting to her closeness.

'The clan can be a bit overwhelming *en masse*,' she said. 'I won't introduce you to everyone by name; it would be unfair to expect you to remember all of them. My mother is Jennifer, my father is Ray. Hannah's husband is Paul.'

'I appreciate that,' he said, tugging at his collar that suddenly seemed too tight. As an only child, he'd always found meeting other people's families intimidating.

Andie gave him a reassuring smile. 'With the Newman family, what you see is what you get. They're all good people who will take you as they find you. We might even get some volunteers to help on Christmas Day out of this.'

The corridor opened out into a spacious open-plan family room. At some time in the last twenty years the parents had obviously added a new extension. It looked dated now but solid—warm and comfortable and welcoming. Delicious aromas emanated from the farmhouse-style kitchen in the northern corner. He sniffed and Andie smiled. 'My mother's lasagne—wait until you taste it.'

She announced him with an encompassing wave of her arm. 'Everyone, this is Dominic. He's a very important new client so please make him welcome. And yes, I know he's gorgeous but it's strictly business between us.'

That was met with laughter and a chorus of 'Hi, Dominic!' and 'Welcome!' Andie then briefly explained to them about the party and Hannah's likely role in it.

There were so many of them. Andie's introduction had guaranteed all eyes were on him. About ten people, including kids, were ranged around the room, sitting in comfortable-looking sofas or around a large trestle table.

Each face came into focus as the adults greeted him with warm smiles. It wasn't difficult to tell who was related—Andie's smile was a strong family marker that originated with her father, a tall, thin man with a vigorous handshake. Her mother's smile was different but equally welcoming as she headed his way from the kitchen, wiping her hands on her apron before she greeted him. Three young children playing on the floor looked up, then kept on playing with their toys. A big black dog with a greying muzzle, lying stretched out near the kids, lifted his head, then thumped his tail in greeting.

Andie's sister Hannah and her husband, Paul, paused in their job of setting the large trestle table to say hello. His experience with social workers in his past had been good—a social worker had pretty much saved his life—and he was not disappointed by Hannah's kind eyes in a gentle face.

'I straight away know of several families who are facing a very grim Christmas indeed,' she said. 'Your generous gesture would make an immense difference to them.'

Andie caught his eye and smiled. Instinctively, he knew she had steered him in the right direction towards her sister. If all Andie's ideas for his party were as good as this one, he could face the

Christmas Day he dreaded with more confidence than he might have expected.

Andie's policy of glaring down any family member who dared to even hint at dating possibilities with Dominic was working. Except for her younger sister, Bea, who could not resist hissing, 'He's hot,' at any opportunity, from passing the salad to refilling her water glass. Then, when Andie didn't bite, Bea added, 'If you don't want him, hand him over to me.' Thankfully, Dominic remained oblivious to the whispered exchanges.

Her family had, unwittingly or not, sat Dominic in the same place at the table where Anthony had sat at these gatherings. *Andie and Ant—always together.* She doubted it was on purpose. Dominic needed to sit between Hannah and her and so it had just happened.

In the years since he'd died, no man had come anywhere near to replacing Anthony in her heart. How could they? Anthony and she had been two halves of the same soul, she sometimes thought. Maybe she would never be able to love anyone else. *But she was lonely.* The kind of loneliness that work, friends, family could not displace.

In the months after Anthony's death her parents had left Anthony's customary seat empty out of respect. Unable to bear the emptiness that emphasised his absence, she had stopped coming to the family dinners until her mother had realised the pain it was causing. From then on, one of her brothers always occupied Anthony's chair.

Now she told herself she was okay with Dominic sitting there. He was only a client, with no claim to any place in her heart. Bringing him along tonight had worked out well—one of those spur-of-the-moment decisions she mightn't have made if she'd given it more thought.

Dominic and Hannah had spent a lot of time talking—but he'd managed to chat with everyone else there too. They were obviously charmed by him. That was okay too. *She* was charmed by him. Tonight she was seeing a side of him, as he interacted with her family, that she might never have seen in everyday business dealings.

Her sister was right. *Dominic was hot.* And Andie was only too aware of it. She was surprised at the fierce urge of possessiveness that swept over her at the thought of 'handing over' Dominic to anyone else. Her sister could find her own hot guy.

Even at the dinner table, when her back was angled away from him to talk to her brother on her other side, she was aware of Dominic. His scent had already become familiar—citrus-sharp yet warm and very masculine. Her ears were tuned into the sound of his voice—no matter where he was in the room. Her body was on constant alert to that attraction, which had been instant and only continued to grow with further contact. On their way in, in the corridor, when she'd drawn close to whisper so her family would not overhear, she'd felt light-headed from the proximity to him.

It had been five years now since Anthony had gone—the same length of time they'd been together. She would never forget him but that terrible grief and anguish she had felt at first had eventually mellowed to a grudging acceptance. She realised she had stopped dreaming about him.

People talked about once-in-a-lifetime love. She'd thought she'd found it at the age of eighteen—and a cruel fate had snatched him away from her. Was there to be only one great love for her?

Deep in her heart, she didn't want to believe that. Surely there would be someone for her again? She didn't want to be alone. One day she wanted marriage, a family. She'd been looking for someone like Anthony—and had been constantly disappointed in the men she'd gone out with. But was it a mistake to keep on looking for a man like her teenage soulmate?

Thoughts of Dominic were constantly invading her mind. He was so different from Anthony there could be no comparison. Anthony had been blond and lean, laidback and funny, always quick with a joke, creative and musical. From what she knew of Dominic, he was quite the opposite. She'd dismissed him as not for her. But her body's reaction kept contradicting her mind's stonewalling. How could she be so certain he was Mr Wrong?

Dessert was being served—spring berries and home-made vanilla bean ice cream—and she turned to Dominic at the precise moment he turned to her. Their eyes connected and held and she knew without the need for words that he was happy with her decision to bring him here.

'Your family is wonderful,' he said in a low undertone.

'I think so,' she said, pleased. 'What about you? Do you come from a large family?'

A shadow darkened his eyes. He shook his head. 'Only child.'

She smiled. 'We must seem overwhelming.'

'In a good way,' he said. 'You're very lucky.'

'I know.' Of course she and her siblings had had the usual squabbles and disagreements throughout their childhood and adolescence. She, as number four, had had to fight for her place. But as adults they all got on as friends as well as brothers and sisters. She couldn't have got through the loss of Anthony without her family's support.

'The kids are cute,' he said. 'So well behaved.'

Her nephews, Timothy and Will, and her niece, Caitlin, were together down the other end of the table under the watchful eye of their grandmother. 'They're really good kids,' she agreed. 'I adore them.'

'Little Timothy seems quite…delicate,' Dominic said, obviously choosing his words carefully. 'But I notice his older cousin looks after him.'

A wave of sadness for Hannah and Paul's little son overwhelmed her. 'They're actually the same age,' she said. 'Both five years old. Timothy just looks as though he's three.'

'I guess I don't know much about kids,' Dominic said, shifting uncomfortably in his chair.

She lowered her voice. 'Sadly, little Timothy has some kind of rare growth disorder, an endocrine imbalance. That's why he's so small.'

Dominic answered in a lowered voice. 'Can it be treated?'

'Only with a new treatment that isn't yet subsidised by the public health system. Even for private treatment, he's on a waiting list.' It was the reason why she drove an old car, why Bea had moved back home to save on rent, why the whole family was pulling together to raise the exorbitant amount of money required for tiny Timothy's private treatment.

But she would not tell Dominic that. While she might be wildly attracted to him, she still had no reason to think he was other than the Scrooge of his reputation. A man who had to be forced into a public display of charity to broker a multi-million-dollar business deal. Not for one moment did she want him to think she might be angling for financial help for Timothy.

'It's all under control,' she said as she passed him a bowl of raspberries.

'I'm glad to hear that,' he said, helping himself to the berries and then the ice cream. 'Thank you for inviting me tonight and for introducing me to Hannah. The next step is for you and your business partners to come in to my headquarters for a meeting with my marketing people. Can the three of you make it on Friday?'

CHAPTER SIX

ANDIE AND HER two business partners, Gemma and Eliza, settled themselves in a small waiting room off the main reception area of Dominic's very plush offices in Circular Quay. She and her fellow Party Queens had just come out of the Friday meeting with Dominic, his marketing people and senior executives in the boardroom and were waiting for Dominic to hear his feedback.

Situated on Sydney Cove, at the northern end of the CBD, the area was not just one of the most popular harbourside tourist precincts in Sydney—it was also home to the most prestigious office buildings. Even in this small room, floor-to-ceiling glass walls gave a magnificent close view of the Sydney Harbour Bridge and a luxury cruise liner in dock.

Andie couldn't help thinking the office was an ideal habitat for a billionaire Scrooge. Then she backtracked on the thought. That might not be fair. He hated the term and she felt vaguely disloyal even thinking it. Dominic was now totally committed to the Christmas Day feast for underprivileged families and had just approved a more than generous budget. She was beginning to wonder if his protestation that he was *not* a Scrooge had some truth in it. And then there was his gift to her mother to consider.

As she pondered the significance of that, she realised her thoughts had been filled with nothing much but Dominic since the day she'd met him. Last night he had even invaded her dreams—in a very passionate encounter that made her blush at the hazy dream memory of it. *Did he kiss like that in real life?*

It was with an effort that she forced her thoughts back to business.

'How do you guys think it went?' she asked the other two. 'My vote is for really well.' She felt jubilant and buoyant—Dominic's team had embraced her idea with more enthusiasm than she could ever have anticipated.

'Considering the meeting was meant to go from ten to eleven and here it is, nearly midday, yes, I think you could say that,' said Eliza with a big smile splitting her face.

'Of course that could have had something to do with Gemma's superb macadamia shortbread and those delectable fruit mince pies,' said Andie.

'Yes,' said Gemma with a pleased smile. 'I thought

I could describe until I was blue in the face what I wanted to serve for the lunch, but they'd only know by tasting it.'

Party Queens' foodie partner had not only come up with a detailed menu for Dominic's Christmas Day lunch, but she'd also brought along freshly baked samples of items from her proposed menus. At the end of the meeting only a few crumbs had remained on the boardroom's fine china plates. Andie had caught Dominic's eye as he finished his second pastry and knew it had been an inspired idea. The Christmas star shaped serviettes she had brought along had also worked to keep the meeting focused on the theme of traditional with a twist.

'I think they were all-round impressed,' said Eliza. 'We three worked our collective socks off to get our presentations so detailed and professional in such a short time. Andie, all the images and samples you prepared to show the decorations and table settings looked amazing—I got excited at how fabulous it's going to look.'

'I loved the idea of the goody bags for all the guests too,' said Gemma. 'You really thought of everything.'

'While we're doing some mutual backslapping I'm giving yours a hearty slap, Eliza,' said Andie. 'Their finance guy couldn't fault your detailed costings and timelines.'

Eliza rubbed her hands together in exaggerated

glee. 'And I'm sure we're going to get more party bookings from them. One of the senior marketing people mentioned her daughter was getting married next year and asked me did we do weddings.'

'Well done, Party Queens,' said Andie. 'Now that the contract is signed and the basic plan approved I feel I can relax.' Her partners had no idea of how tight it had been to get Dominic across the line for the change from glitz and glamour to more humble with heart.

She and her two friends discreetly high-fived each other. The room was somewhat of a goldfish bowl and none of them wanted to look less than professional to any of Dominic's staff who might be walking by.

Eliza leaned in to within whispering distance of Andie and Gemma. 'Dominic Hunt was a surprise,' she said in an undertone. 'I thought he'd be arrogant and overbearing. Instead, I found myself actually liking him.'

'Me too,' said Gemma. 'Not to mention he's so handsome. I could hardly keep my eyes off him. And that voice.' She mimed a shiver of delight.

'But *he* couldn't keep his eyes off Andie,' said Eliza. 'You'd be wasting your time there, Gemma.'

Had he? Been unable to keep his eyes off her? Andie's Dominic radar had been on full alert all through the meeting. Again she'd that uncanny experience of knowing exactly where he was in the room even when her back was turned. Of hearing his voice through the chatter of others. She'd caught his eye one too many times to feel comfortable. Especially with the remnants of that dream lingering in her mind. She'd had to force herself not to let her gaze linger on his mouth.

'Really, Andie?' said Gemma. 'Has he asked you out?'

'Nothing like that,' Andie said.

Eliza nodded thoughtfully. 'But you like him. Not in the way I liked him. I mean you *really* like him.'

Andie had no intention of admitting anything to anyone. She forced her voice to sound cool, impartial—though she doubted she would fool shrewd Eliza. 'Like you, I was surprised at how easy he is to get on with and how professional he is—even earlier this week when I switched the whole concept of his party into something he had never envisaged.' That overwhelming attraction was just physical—nothing more.

'And you totally didn't get how hot he was?' said Gemma. 'Don't expect me to believe that for one moment.'

Eliza rolled her eyes at Andie. 'I know what's coming next. *He's not your type.* How many times have I heard you say that when you either refuse a date or dump a guy before you've even had a chance to get to know him?'

Andie paused. 'Maybe that's true. Maybe that's why I'm still single. I'm beginning to wonder if I really know what *is* my type now.'

Her friendships with Gemma and Eliza dated from after she'd lost Anthony. They'd been sympathetic, but never really got why she had been so determined to try and find another man cast in the same mould as her first love. That her first love had been so perfect she'd felt her best chance of happiness would be with someone like Anthony.

Trouble was, they'd broken the mould when they'd made Anthony. Maybe she just hadn't been ready. Maybe she'd been subconsciously avoiding any man who might challenge her. Or might force her to look at why she'd put her heart on hold for so long. *Dominic would be a challenge in every way.* The thought both excited and scared her.

Eliza shook her head. 'It's irrelevant anyway,' she said. 'It would be most unwise for you to start anything with Dominic Hunt. His party is a big, important job for us and we don't have much time to organise it. It could get very messy if you started dating the client. Especially when I've never known you to stay with anyone for more than two weeks.'

'In my eagerness to get you fixed up with a handsome rich guy, I hadn't thought of that,' said Gemma. 'Imagine if you broke up with the billionaire client right in the middle of the countdown to the event. Could get awkward.'

'It's not going to happen, girls,' Andie said. 'I won't lie and say I don't think he's really attractive. But that's as far as it goes.' Thinking of last night's very intimate dream, she crossed her fingers behind her back.

'This is a huge party for us to pull together so quickly. We've got other jobs to get sorted as well. I can't afford to get...distracted.' How she actually stopped herself from getting distracted by Dominic was another matter altogether.

'I agree,' said Eliza. 'Eyes off the client. Okay?'

Andie smiled. 'I'll try,' she said. 'Seriously, though, it's really important for Dominic that this party works. He's got a lot riding on it. And it's really important for us. As you say, Eliza, more work could come from this. Not just weddings and private parties. But why not his company's business functions too? We have to think big.'

Gemma giggled. 'Big? Mr Hunt is way too big for me anyway. He's so tall. And all those muscles. His face is handsome but kind of tough too, don't you think?'

'Shh,' hissed Eliza, putting her finger to her lips. 'He's coming.'

Andie screwed up her eyes for a moment. How mortifying if he'd caught them gossiping about him. She'd been just about to say he wasn't too big for her to handle.

Along with the other two, she looked up and straightened her shoulders as Dominic strode towards them. In his dark charcoal suit he looked every inch the billionaire businessman. And, yes, very big.

She caught her breath at how handsome he looked. At the same time she caught his eye. And got the distinct impression that, of the three women in the room, she was the only one he really saw.

Did Andie get more and more beautiful every time he saw her? Dominic wondered. Or was it just the more he got to know her, the more he liked and admired her?

He had been impressed by her engaging and professional manner in the boardroom—the more so because he was aware she'd had such a short time to prepare her presentation. Her two business partners had been impressive too. It took a lot to win over his hard-nosed marketing people but, as a team, Party Queens had bowled them over.

The three women got up from their seats as he approached. Andie, tall and elegant in a deceptively simple caramel-coloured short dress—businesslike but with a snug fit that showed off her curves. Her sensational legs seemed to go on for ever to end in sky-high leopard-skin-print stilettos. He got it. She wanted to look business-like but also let it be known who was the creative mind behind Party Queens. It worked.

Gemma—shorter, curvier, with auburn hair—and sophisticated, dark-haired Eliza were strikingly attractive too. They had a glint in their eyes and humour in their smiles that made him believe they could enjoy a party as well as plan them. But, in his eyes, Andie outshone them. Would any other woman ever be able to beat her? It was disturbing that a woman who he had known for such a short time could have made such an impression on him.

He addressed all three, while being hyper aware of Andie as he did so. Her hair pulled back in a loose knot that fell in soft tendrils around her face, her mouth slicked with coral gloss, those remarkable green eyes. 'As I'm sure you're aware,' he began, 'my marketing team is delighted at both the concept for the party and the way you plan to implement the concept to the timeline. They're confident the event will meet and exceed the target we've set for reputation management and positive media engagement.'

It sounded like jargon and he knew it. But how else could he translate the only real aim of the party: to make him look less the penny-pincher and more the philanthropist?

'We're very pleased to be working with such a professional team,' said Eliza, the business brains of the partnership. But all three were business savvy in their own way, he'd realised through the meeting.

'Thank you,' he said. He glanced at his watch. 'The meeting ran so late it's almost lunchtime. I'm extending an invitation to lunch for all of you,' he said. 'Not that restaurants around here, excellent as they are, could match the standard of your cooking, Gemma.'

'Thank you,' said Gemma, looking pleased. 'But I'm afraid I have an appointment elsewhere.'

'Me too, and I'm running late,' said Eliza. 'But we couldn't possibly let you lunch alone, Mr Hunt, could we, Andie?'

Andie flushed high on those elegant cheekbones. 'Of course not. I'd be delighted to join Dominic for lunch.'

Her chin tilted upwards and he imagined her friends might later be berated for landing her in this on her own. Not that he minded. The other women were delightful, but lunch one-on-one with Andie was his preferred option.

'There are a few details of the plan I need to finalise with Dominic anyway,' she said to her friends.

Dominic shook hands with Gemma and Eliza and they headed towards the elevators. He turned to Andie. 'Thank you for coming to lunch with me,' he said.

She smiled. 'Be warned, I'm starving. I was up at the crack of dawn finalising those mood boards for the presentation.'

'They were brilliant. There's only one thing I'd like to see changed. I didn't want to mention it in the meeting as it's my personal opinion and I didn't want to have to debate it.'

She frowned, puzzled rather than worried, he thought. 'Yes?'

He put his full authority behind his voice—he would not explain his reasons. Ever. 'The Christmas tree. The big one you have planned for next to the staircase. I don't want it.'

'Sure,' she said, obviously still puzzled. 'I thought it would be wonderful to have the tree where it's the first thing the guests see, but I totally understand if you don't want it there. We can put the Christmas tree elsewhere. The living room. Even in the area near where we'll be eating. Wherever you suggest.'

He hadn't expected this to be easy—he knew everyone would expect to see a decorated tree on Christmas Day. 'You misunderstood me. I mean I don't want a Christmas tree anywhere. No tree at all in my house.'

She paused. He could almost see her internal debate reflected in the slight crease between her eyebrows, the barely visible pursing of her lips. But then she obviously thought it was not worth the battle. 'Okay,' she said with a shrug of her slender shoulders. 'No tree.'

'Thank you,' he said, relieved he wasn't going to have to further assert his authority. At this time of year, Christmas trees were appearing all over the place. He avoided them when he could. But he would never have a tree in his home—a constant reminder of the pain and loss and guilt associated with the festive season.

They walked together to the elevator. When it arrived, there were two other people in it. They got out two floors below. Then Dominic was alone in the confined space of the elevator, aware of Andie's closeness, her warm scent. What was it? Sandalwood? Something exotic and sensual. He had the craziest impulse to hold her closer so he could nuzzle into the softness of her throat, the better to breathe it in.

He clenched his fists beside him and moved as far as he could away from her so his shoulder hit the wall of the elevator. That would be insanity. And probably not the best timing when he'd just quashed her Christmas tree display.

But she wouldn't be Andie if she didn't persevere. 'Not even miniature trees on the lunch table?' she asked.

'No trees,' he said.

She sighed. 'Okay, the client has spoken. No Christmas tree.'

The elevator came to the ground floor. He lightly placed his hand at the small of her back to steer her in the direction of the best exit for the restaurant. Bad idea. Touching Andie even in this casual manner just made him want to touch her more.

'But you're happy with the rest of the plan?' she said as they walked side by side towards the restaurant, dodging the busy Sydney lunchtime crush as they did.

'Very happy. Except you can totally discard the marketing director's suggestion I dress up as Santa Claus.'

She laughed. 'Did you notice I wrote it down but didn't take the suggestion any further?' Her eyes narrowed as she looked him up and down in mock inspection. 'Though it's actually a nice idea. If you change your mind—'

'No,' he said.

'That's what I thought,' she said, that delightful smile dancing around the corners of her mouth.

'You know it's been a stretch for me to agree to a Christmas party at all. You won't ever see me as Santa.'

'What if the marketing director himself could be convinced to play Santa Claus?' she said thoughtfully. 'He volunteered to help out on the day.'

'This whole party thing was Rob Cratchit's idea so that might be most appropriate. Take it as an order from his boss.'

'I'll send him an email and say it's your suggestion,' she said with a wicked grin. 'He's quite well padded and would make a wonderful Santa—no pillow down the front of his jacket required.'

'Don't mention that in the email or all hell will break loose,' he said.

'Don't worry; I can be subtle when I want to,' she said, that grin still dancing in her eyes as they neared the restaurant.

In Dominic's experience, some restaurants were sited well and had a good fit-out; others had excellent food. In this case, his favourite place to eat near the office had both—a spectacular site on the top of a heritage listed building right near the water and a superlative menu.

There had been no need to book—a table was always there for him when he wanted one, no matter how long the waiting list for bookings.

An attentive waiter settled Andie into a seat facing the view of Sydney Harbour. 'I've always wanted to eat at this restaurant,' she said, looking around her.

'Maybe we should have our meetings here in future?'

'Good idea,' she said. 'Though I'll have to do a detailed site inspection of your house very soon. We could fit in a meeting then, perhaps?'

'I might not be able to be there,' he said. 'I have a series of appointments in other states over the next two weeks. Any meetings with you might have to be via the Internet.'

Was that disappointment he saw cloud her eyes. 'That's a shame. I—'

'My assistant will help you with access and the security code,' he said. He wished he could cancel some of the meetings, but that was not possible. Perhaps it was for the best. The more time he spent with Andie, the more he wanted to break his rules and ask her on a date. But those rules were there for good reason.

'As you know, we have a tight timeline to work to,' she said. 'The more we get done early the better, to allow for the inevitable last-minute dramas.'

'I have every confidence in you that it will go to plan.'

'Me too,' she said with another of those endearing grins. 'I've organised so many Christmas room sets and table settings for magazine and advertising clients. You have to get creative to come up with something different each year. This is easier in a way.'

'But surely there must be a continuity?' he asked, curious even though Christmas was his least favourite topic of conversation.

'Some people don't want to go past traditional red and green and that's okay,' she said. 'I've done an entire room themed purple and the client was delighted. Silver and gold is always popular in

Australia, when Christmas is likely to be sweltering—it seems to feel cooler somehow. But—'

The waiter came to take their orders. They'd been too busy talking to look at the menu. Quickly they discussed their favourites before they ordered: barramundi with prawns and asparagus for him; tandoori roasted ocean trout with cucumber salsa for her and an heirloom tomato salad to share. They each passed on wine and chose mineral water. 'Because it's a working day,' they both said at the exact time and laughed. *It felt like a date.* He could not let his thoughts stray that way. Because he liked the idea too much.

'You haven't explained the continuity of Christmas,' he said, bringing the conversation back to the party.

'It's nothing to do with the baubles and the tinsel and everything to do with the feeling,' she said with obvious enthusiasm. 'Anticipation, delight, joy. For some it's about religious observance, spirituality and new life; others about sharing and generosity. If you can get people feeling the emotion, then it doesn't really matter if the tree is decorated in pink and purple or red and green.'

How about misery and fear and pain? Those were his memories of Christmas. 'I see your point,' he said.

'I intend to make sure your party is richly imbued with that kind of Christmas spirit. Hannah told me some of the kids who will be coming would be unlikely to have a celebration meal or a present and certainly not both if it wasn't for your generosity.'

'I met with Hannah yesterday; she mentioned how important it will be for the families we're inviting. She seems to think the party will do a powerful lot of good. Your sister told me how special Christmas is in your family.' It was an effort for him to speak about Christmas in a normal tone of voice. But he seemed to be succeeding.

'Oh, yes,' said Andie. 'Heaven help anyone who might want to celebrate it with their in-laws or anywhere else but my parents' house.'

'Your mother's a marvellous cook.'

'True, but Christmas is well and truly my dad's day. My mother is allowed to do the baking and she does that months in advance. On the day, he cooks a traditional meal—turkey, ham, roast beef, the lot. He's got favourite recipes he's refined over the years and no one would dare suggest anything different.'

Did she realise how lucky she was? How envious he felt when he thought about how empty his life had been of the kind of family love she'd been gifted with. He'd used to think he could start his own family, his own traditions, but his ex-wife had disabused him of that particular dream. It involved trust and trust was not a thing that came easily to him. Not when it came to women. 'I can't imagine you would want to change a tradition.'

'If truth be told, we'd be furious if he wanted to change one little thing,' she said, her voice warm with affection for her father. *She knew.*

He could see where she got her confidence from—that rock-solid security of a loving, supportive family. But now he knew she'd been tempered by tragedy too. He wanted to know more about how she had dealt with the loss of her boyfriend. But not until it was appropriate to ask.

'What about you, Dominic—did you celebrate Christmas with your family?' she asked.

This never got easier—which was why he chose not to revisit it too often. 'My parents died when I was eleven,' he said.

'Oh, I'm so sorry,' she said with warm compassion in her eyes. 'What a tragedy.' She paused. 'You were so young, an only child…who looked after you?'

'We lived in England, in a village in Norfolk. My father was English, my mother Australian. My mother's sister was staying with us at the time my parents died. She took me straight back with her to Australia.' It was difficult to keep his voice matter of fact, not to betray the pain the memories evoked, even after all this time.

'What? Just wrenched you away from your home?' She paused. 'I'm sorry. That wasn't my call to say that. You were lucky you had family. Did your aunt have children?'

'No, it was just the two of us,' he said and left it at that. There was so much more he could say about the toxic relationship with his aunt but that was part of his past he'd rather was left buried.

Wrenched. That was how it had been. Away from everything familiar. Away from his grandparents, whom he didn't see again until he had the wherewithal to get himself back to the UK as an adult. Away from the dog he'd adored. Desperately lonely and not allowed to grieve, thrust back down in Brisbane, in the intense heat, straight into the strategic battleground that was high school in a foreign country. To a woman who had no idea how to love a child, though she had tried in her own warped way.

'I'd prefer not to talk about it,' he said. 'I'm all grown up now and don't angst about the past.' Except when it was dark and lonely and he couldn't sleep and he wondered if he was fated to live alone without love.

'I understand,' she said. But how could she?

She paused to leave a silence he did not feel able to fill.

'Talking about my family,' she finally said, 'you're my mother's new number one favourite person.'

Touched by not only her words but her effort to

draw him in some way into her family circle, he smiled. 'And why is that?'

'Seriously, she really liked you at dinner on Wednesday night. But then, when you had flowers delivered the next day, she was over the moon. Especially at the note that said she cooked the best lasagne you'd ever tasted.'

'I'm glad she liked them. And it was true about the lasagne.' Home-made anything was rarely on the menu for him so he had appreciated it.

'How did you know pink was her favourite colour in flowers?'

'I noticed the flowers she'd planted in her garden.'

'But you only saw the garden so briefly.'

'I'm observant,' he said.

'But the icing on the cake was the voucher for dinner for two at their local bistro.'

'She mentioned she liked their food when we were talking,' he said.

'You're a thoughtful guy, aren't you?' she said, tilting her head to the side.

'Some don't think so,' he said, unable to keep the bitterness from his voice.

She lowered her voice to barely a whisper so he had to lean across the table to hear her, so close their heads were touching. Anyone who was watching would think they *were* on a date.

She placed her hand on his arm in a gesture of

comfort which touched him. 'Don't worry. The party should change all that. I really liked Rob's idea that no media would be invited to the party. That journalists would have to volunteer to help on the day if they wanted to see what it was all about.'

'And no photographers allowed, to preserve our guests' privacy. I liked that too.'

'I really have a good feeling about it,' she said. She lifted her hand off his arm and he felt bereft of her touch.

He nodded. If it were up to him, if he didn't *have* to go ahead with the party, he'd cancel it at a moment's notice. Maybe there was a touch of Scrooge in him after all.

But he didn't want Andie to think that of him. Not for a moment.

He hadn't proved to be a good judge of women. His errors in judgement went right back to his aunt—he'd loved her when she was his fun auntie from Australia. She'd turned out to be a very different person. Then there'd been Melody—sweet, doomed Melody. At seventeen he'd been a man in body but a boy still in heart. He'd been gutted at her betrayal, too damn wet behind the ears to re-alise a teenage boy's love could never be enough for an addict. Then how could he have been sucked in by Tara? His ex-wife was a redhead like Melody, tiny and delicate. But her frail exterior hid an avaricious, dishonest heart and she had lied to him about something so fundamental to their marriage that he could never forgive her.

Now there was Andie. He didn't trust his feelings when he'd made such disastrous calls before. *'What you see is what you get,'* she'd said about her family.

Could he trust himself to judge that Andie was what she appeared to be?

He reined in his errant thoughts—he only needed to trust Andie to deliver him the party he needed to improve his public image. Anything personal was not going to happen.

CHAPTER SEVEN

'ANDIE, I NEED to see you.' Dominic's voice on her smartphone was harsh in its urgency. It was eight a.m. and Andie had not been expecting a call from him. He'd been away more than a week on business and she'd mainly communicated with him by text and email—and only then if it was something that needed his approval for the party. The last time she'd seen him was the Friday they'd had lunch together. The strictly business lunch that had somehow felt more like a date. But she couldn't let herself think like that.

'Sure,' she said. 'I just have to—'

'Now. Please. Where do you live?'

Startled at his tone, she gave him the address of the apartment in a converted warehouse in the inner western suburb of Newtown she shared with two old schoolfriends. Her friends had both already left for work. Andie had planned on a day finalising prop hire and purchase for Dominic's party before she started work for a tuxedo-and-tiara-themed twenty-first birthday party.

She quickly changed into skinny denim jeans and a simple loose-knit cream top that laced with leather ties at the neckline. Decided on her favourite leopard-print stilettos over flats. And make-up. And her favourite sandalwood and jasmine perfume. What the heck—her heart was racing at the thought of seeing him. She didn't want to seem as though she were trying too hard—but then again she didn't want to be caught out in sweats.

When Dominic arrived she was shocked to see he didn't look *his* sartorial best. In fact he looked downright dishevelled. His black hair seemed as if he'd used his fingers for a comb and his dark stubble was one step away from a beard. He was wearing black jeans, a dark grey T-shirt and had a black leather jacket slung over his shoulders. Immediately he owned the high-ceilinged room, a space that overwhelmed men of lesser stature, with the casual athleticism of his stance, the power of his body with its air of tightly coiled energy.

'Are you alone?' he asked.

'Yes,' she said. *Yes!*

Her first thought was that he looked hotter than ever—so hot she had to catch her breath. This Dominic set her pulse racing even more than executive Dominic in his made-to-measure Italian suits.

Her second thought was that he seemed stressed—his mouth set in a grim line, his eyes red-rimmed and darkly shadowed. 'Are you okay?' she asked.

'I've come straight from the airport. I just flew in from Perth.' Perth was on the other side of Australia—a six-hour flight. 'I cut short my trip.'

'But are you okay?' She forced her voice to sound calm and measured, not wanting him to realise how she was reacting to his untamed good looks. Her heart thudded with awareness that they were alone in the apartment.

With the kind of friendly working relationship they had now established, it would be quite in order to greet him with a light kiss on his beard-roughened cheek. But she wouldn't dare. She might not be able to resist sliding her mouth across his cheek to his mouth and turning it into a very different kind of kiss. And that wouldn't do.

'I'm fine. I've just…been presented with…with a dilemma,' Dominic said.

'Coffee might help,' she said.

'Please.'

'Breakfast? I have—'

'Just coffee.'

But Andie knew that sometimes men who said they didn't want anything to eat needed food. And that their mood could improve immeasurably when they ate something. Not that she'd been in the habit of sharing breakfast with a man. Not since… She forced her mind back to the present and away from memories of breakfasts with Anthony on a sun-soaked veranda. Her memories of him were lit with sunshine and happiness.

Dominic dragged out a chair and slumped down at her kitchen table while she prepared him coffee. *Why was he here?* She turned to see him with his elbows on the tabletop, resting his head on his hands. Tired? Defeated? Something seemed to have put a massive dent in his usual self-assured confidence.

She slid a mug of coffee in front of him. 'I assumed black but here's frothed milk and sugar if you want.'

'Black is what I need,' he said. He put both hands around the mug and took it to his mouth.

Without a word, she put a thick chunk of fresh fruit bread, studded with figs and apricots, from her favourite baker in King Street in front of him. Then a dish of cream cheese and a knife. 'Food might help,' she said.

He put down his coffee, gave her a weary imitation of his usual glower and went to pick up the bread. 'Let me,' she said and spread it with cream cheese.

What was it about this man that made her want to comfort and care for him? He was a thirty-two-year-old billionaire, for heaven's sake. Tough, self-sufficient. Wealthier than she could even begin to imagine. And yet she sometimes detected an air of vulnerability about him that wrenched at her. A sense of something broken. But it was not up to her to try and fix him. He ate the fruit bread in two bites. 'More?' she asked.

He nodded. 'It's good,' he said.

Andie had to be honest with herself. She wanted to comfort him, yes. She enjoyed his company. But it was more than that. She couldn't deny that compelling physical attraction. He sat at her kitchen table, his leather jacket slung on the back of the chair. His tanned arms were sculpted with muscle, his T-shirt moulded ripped pecs and abs. With his rough-hewn face, he looked so utterly *male*.

Desire, so long unfamiliar, thrilled through her. She wanted to kiss him and feel those strong arms around her, his hands on her body. *She wanted more than kisses.* What was it about this not-my-type man who had aroused her interest from the moment she'd first met him?

When he'd eaten two more slices of fruit bread, he pushed his plate away and leaned back in his seat. His sigh was weary and heartfelt. 'Thank you,' he said. 'I didn't realise I was hungry.'

She slipped into the chair opposite him and nursed her own cooling cup of coffee to stop the impulse to reach over and take his hand. 'Are you able to tell me about your dilemma?' she asked, genuinely concerned.

He raked his hands through his hair. 'My ex-wife is causing trouble. Again.'

In her research into Dominic, Andie had seen photos of Tara Hunt—she still went by his name—a petite, pale-skinned redhead in designer clothes and an over-abundance of jewellery.

'I'm sorry,' she said, deciding on caution in her reaction. 'Do you want to tell me about it?' Was that why he wanted to see her? To cry on her shoulder about his ex-wife? Dominic didn't seem like a crying-on-shoulders kind of guy.

He went to drink more coffee, to find his mug was nearly empty. He drained the last drops. 'You make good coffee,' he said appreciatively.

'I worked as a barista when I was a student,' she said.

She and Anthony had both worked in hospitality, saving for vacation backpacker trips to Indonesia and Thailand. It seemed so long ago now, those days when she took it for granted they had a long, happy future stretched out ahead of them. They'd been saving for a trip to Eastern Europe when he'd died.

She took Dominic's mug from him, got up, refilled it, brought it back to the table and sat down again. He drank from it and put it down.

Dominic leaned across the table to bring him closer to her. 'Can I trust you, Andie?' he asked in that deep, resonant voice. His intense grey gaze met hers and held it.

'Of course,' she said without hesitation.

He sat back in his chair. 'I know you're friends with journalists, so I have to be sure what I might talk to you about today won't go any further.' The way he said it didn't sound offensive; in fact it made her feel privileged that he would consider her trustworthy. Not to mention curious about what he might reveal.

'I assure you, you can trust me,' she said.

'Thank you,' he said. 'Tara found out about my impending deal with Walter Burton and is doing her best to derail it.'

Andie frowned. 'How can she do that?'

'Before I married Tara, she worked for my company in the accounts department. She made it her business to find out everything she could about the way I ran things. I didn't know, but once I started dating her she used that knowledge to make trouble, hiding behind the shield of our relationship. None of my staff dared tell me.'

'Not good,' Andie said, wanting to express in no uncertain terms what she thought of his ex, yet not wanting to get into a bitching session about her.

'You're right about that,' he said. 'It's why I now never date employees.'

His gaze met hers again and held it for a long moment. Was there a message in there for her?

If she wasn't a contractor, would he ask her out? If she hadn't promised her partners to stay away from him, would she suggest a date?

'That policy makes…sense,' she said. What about after Christmas, when she and Dominic would no longer be connected by business? Could they date then? A sudden yearning for that to happen surprised her with its intensity. *She wanted him.*

'It gets worse,' he continued. 'A former employee started his own business in competition with me—' Andie went to protest but Dominic put up his hand. 'It happens; that's legit,' he said. 'But what happened afterwards wasn't. After our marriage broke up, Tara used her knowledge of how my company worked to help him.'

Andie couldn't help her gasp of outrage. 'Did her…her betrayal work?'

'She gave him the information. That didn't mean he knew how to use it. But now I've just discovered she's working with him in a last-minute rival bid for the joint venture with Walter Burton.'

Andie shook her head in disbelief. 'Why?' Her research had shown her Tara Hunt had ended up with a massive divorce settlement from Dominic. Per day of their short marriage, she had walked away with an incredible number of dollars.

Dominic shrugged. 'Revenge. Spite. Who knows what else?'

'Surely Walter Burton won't be swayed by that kind of underhand behaviour?'

'Traditional values are important to Walter Burton. We know that. That's why we're holding the party to negate the popular opinion of me as a Scrooge.'

'So what does your ex-wife have to do with the deal?'

Dominic sighed, a great weary sigh that made Andie want to put comforting arms around him. She'd sensed from the get-go he was a private person. He obviously hated talking about this. Once more, she wondered why he had chosen to.

He drew those dark brows together in a scowl. 'Again she's raked over the coals of our disastrous marriage and talked to her media buddies. Now she's claiming I was unfaithful—which is a big fat lie. According to her, I'm a womaniser, a player and a complete and utter bastard. She dragged out my old quote that I will never marry again and claims it's because I'm incapable of settling with one woman. It's on one of the big Internet gossip sites and will be all over the weekend newspapers.' He cursed under his breath.

Andie could see the shadow of old hurts on his face. He had once loved his ex enough to marry her. A betrayal like this must be painful, no matter how much time had elapsed. She had no such angst behind her. She knew Anthony had been loyal to her, as she had been to him. *First love.* Sometimes she wondered if they might have grown apart if he'd lived. Some of their friends who had dated as teenagers had split when they got older. But she dismissed those thoughts as disloyal to his memory.

Andie shook her head at Dominic's revelations about his ex—it got worse and worse. 'That's horrible—but can't you just ignore it?'

'I would ignore it, but she's made sure Walter Burton has seen all her spurious allegations set out as truth.'

Andie frowned. 'Surely your personal life is none of Mr Burton's business? Especially when it's not true.' She believed Dominic implicitly—why, she wasn't completely sure. Trust went both ways.

'He might think it's true. The *"bed-hopping billionaire"*,' the article calls me.' Dominic growled with wounded outrage. 'That might be enough for Burton to reconsider doing business with me.'

Andie had to put her hand over her mouth to hide her smile at the description.

But Dominic noticed and scowled. 'I know it sounds ludicrous, but to a moralistic family man like Walter Burton it makes me sound immoral and not the kind of guy he wants to do business with.'

'Why do you care so much about the deal with Mr Burton? If you have to pretend to be someone you're not, how can it be worth it?'

'You mean I should pretend *not* to be a bed-hopping billionaire?'

'You must admit the headline has a certain ring to it,' Andie said, losing her battle to keep a straight face.

That forced a reluctant grin from him. 'A tag like that might be very difficult to live down.'

'Is…is it true? Are you a bed-hopping guy?' She held her breath for his reply.

'No. Of course I've had girlfriends since my divorce. Serial monogamy, I think they call it. But nothing like what this scurrilous interview with my ex claims.'

Andie let out her breath on a sigh of relief. 'But do you actually need to pursue this deal if it's becoming so difficult? You're already very wealthy.'

Dominic's mouth set in a grim line. 'I'm not going to bore you with my personal history. But home life with my aunt was less than ideal. I finished high school and got out. I'd tried to run away before and she'd dragged me back. This time she let me go. I ended up homeless, living in a squat. At seventeen I saw inexplicably awful things a boy that age should never see. I never again want to be without money and have nowhere to live. That's all I intend to say about that.' He nodded to her. 'And I trust you not to repeat it.'

'Of course,' she said, rocked by his revelations, aching to know more. *Dominic Hunt was a street kid?* Not boring. There was so much more about his life than he was saying. She thought again about his scarred knuckles and broken nose. There had been nothing about his past in her on-line trawling. She hoped he might tell her more. It seemed he was far more complex than he appeared. Which only made him more attractive.

'My best friend and first business partner, Jake Marlow, is also in with me on this,' he said. 'He wants it as much as I do, for his own reasons I'm not at liberty to share.'

'Okay,' she said slowly. 'So we're working on the party to negate the Scr...uh...the other reputation, to get Mr Burton on board. What do you intend to do about the bed-hopper one?'

'When Burton contacted me I told him that it was all scuttlebutt and I was engaged to be married.'

She couldn't help a gasp. 'You're engaged?' She felt suddenly stricken. 'Engaged to who?'

'I'm not engaged. I'm not even dating anyone.'

'Then why...?' she said.

He groaned. 'Panic. Fear. Survival. A gut reaction like I used to have back in that squat. When you woke up, terrified, in your cardboard box to find some older guy burrowing through your backpack and you told him you had nothing worth stealing even though there was five dollars folded tiny between your toes in your sock. If that money was stolen, you didn't eat.'

'So you lied to Mr Burton?'

'As I said, a panic reaction. But it gets worse.' Again he raked his fingers through his hair. 'Burton said he was flying in to Sydney in two weeks' time to meet with both me and the other guy. He wants to be introduced to my fiancée.'

Andie paused, stunned at what Dominic had done, appalled that he had lied. 'What will you do?'

Again he leaned towards her over the table. 'I want you to be my fiancée, Andie.'

CHAPTER EIGHT

DOMINIC WATCHED ANDIE'S reactions flit across her face—shock and indignation followed by disappointment. In him? He braced himself—certain she was going to say *no*.

'Are you serious?' she finally said, her hands flat down on the table in front of her.

'Very,' he said, gritting his teeth. He'd been an idiot to get himself into a mess like this. *Panic.* He shouldn't have given in to panic in that phone call with Walter Burton. He hadn't let panic or fear rule him for a long time.

Andie tilted her head to one side and frowned. 'You want me to *marry* you? We hardly know each other.'

Marriage? Who was talking about marriage? 'No. Just to *pretend*—' Whatever he said wasn't going to sound good. 'Pretend to be my fiancée. Until after the Christmas party.'

Andie shook her head in disbelief. 'To pretend to be engaged to you? To lie? No! I can't believe you asked me to…to even think of such a thing. I'm a party planner, not a…a…the type of person who would agree to that.'

She looked at him as though she'd never seen him before. And that maybe she didn't like what she saw. Dominic swallowed hard—he didn't like the feeling her expression gave him. She pushed herself up from the chair and walked away from the table, her body rigid with disapproval. He was very aware she wanted to distance herself from him. He didn't like that either. It had seemed so intimate, drinking coffee and eating breakfast at her table. And he *had* liked that.

He swivelled in his chair to face her. 'It was a stupid thing to do, I know that,' he said. He had spent the entire flight back from Perth regretting his impulsive action. 'But it's done.'

She turned around, glared at him. 'Then I suggest you undo it.'

'By admitting I lied?'

She shrugged. 'Tell Mr Burton your fiancée dumped you.'

'As if that would fly.'

'You think it's beyond belief that a woman would ever dump you?'

'I didn't say that.' Though it was true. Since it had ended with Melody, he had always been the one to end a relationship. 'It would seem too… sudden.'

'Just like the sudden engagement?'

'It wouldn't denote...stability.'

'You're right about that.' She crossed her arms in front of her chest—totally unaware that the action pushed up her breasts into an enticing cleavage in the V-necked top she wore. 'It's a crazy idea.'

'I'm not denying that,' he growled. He didn't need to have his mistake pointed out to him. 'But I'm asking you to help me out.'

'Why me? Find someone else. I'm sure there would be no shortage of candidates.'

'But it makes sense for my fiancée to be you.' He could be doggedly persistent when he wanted to be.

He unfolded himself from the too-small chair at the kitchen table. Most chairs were too small for him. He took a step towards her, only for her to take a step back from him. 'Andie. Please.'

Her hair had fallen across her face and she tossed it back. 'Why? We're just client and contractor.'

'Is that all it is between us?'

'Of course it is.' But she wouldn't meet his gaze and he felt triumphant. *So she felt it too.* That attraction that had flashed between them from the get-go.

'When I opened the door to the beautiful woman with the misbehaving skirt—' that got a grudging smile from her '—I thought it could be more than just a business arrangement. But you know now why I don't date anyone hired by the company.'

'And Party Queens has a policy of not mixing business with…with pleasure.' Her voice got huskier on the last words.

He looked her direct in the face, pinning her with his gaze. 'If it ever happened, it would be pleasure all the way, Andie, I think we both know that.' She hadn't quite cleared her face of a wisp of flyaway hair. He reached down and gently smoothed it back behind her ear.

She trembled under his touch. A blush travelled up her throat to stain her cheeks. 'I've never even thought about it, the…the *pleasure,* I mean,' she said.

She wouldn't blush like that if she hadn't. Or flutter her hands to the leather laces of her neckline. *Now who was lying?*

She took a deep breath and he tried to keep his gaze from the resulting further exposure of her cleavage. 'I don't want to be involved in this mad scheme in any way,' she said. 'Except to add your pretend fiancée—when you find one—to the Christmas party guest list.'

'I'm afraid you're already involved.'

She frowned. 'What do you mean?'

Dominic took the few steps necessary back to his chair and took out his smartphone from the inside pocket of his leather jacket. He scrolled through, then handed it to Andie.

She stared at the screen. 'But this is me. *Us.*'

The photo she was staring at was of him and her at a restaurant table. They were leaning towards each other, looking into each other's faces, Andie's hand on his arm.

'At the restaurant in Circular Quay, the day of the Friday meeting,' she said.

'Yes,' he said. The business lunch that had felt like a date. In this photo, it *looked* like a date.

She shook her head, bewildered. 'Who took it?'

'Some opportunistic person with a smartphone, I expect. Maybe a trouble-making friend of Tara's. Who knows?'

She looked back down at the screen, did some scrolling of her own. He waited for her to notice the words that accompanied the image on the gossip site.

Her eyes widened in horror. 'Did you see this?' She read out the heading. *'"Is This the Bed-Hopping Billionaire's New Conquest?"'* She swore under her breath—the first time he had heard her do so.

'I'm sorry. Of course I had no idea this was happening. But, in light of it, you can see why it makes sense that my fake fiancée should be you.'

She shook her head. 'No. It doesn't make any

sense. That was a business lunch. Not the…the romantic rendezvous it appears to be in the picture.'

'You know that. I know that. But the way they've cropped the photo, that's exactly what it seems. Announce an engagement and suddenly the picture would make a whole lot of sense. Good sense.'

Her green eyes narrowed. 'This photo doesn't bother me. It will blow over. We're both single. Who even cares?' He'd been stunned to see the expression in his eyes as he'd looked into her face in the photo. It had looked as if he wanted to have her for dessert. Had she noticed? No wonder the gossip site had drawn a conclusion of romantic intrigue.

'If you're so indifferent, why not help me out?' he said. 'Be my fake fiancée, just until after Christmas.'

'Christmas is nearly a month away. Twenty-five days, to be precise. For twenty-five days I'd have to pretend to be your fiancée?'

'So you're considering it? Because we've already been "outed", so to speak, it wouldn't come out of the blue. It would be believable.'

'Huh! We've only known each other for two weeks. Who would believe it?'

'People get married on less acquaintance,' he said.

'Not people like me,' she said.

'You don't think anyone would believe you

could be smitten by me in that time? I think I'm offended.'

'Of course not,' she said. 'I... I believe many women would be smitten by you. You're handsome, intelligent—'

'And personable, yes, you said. Though I bet you don't think I'm so personable right now.'

She glared at him, though there was a lilt to the corners of her mouth that made it seem like she might want to smile. 'You could be right about that.'

'Now to you—gorgeous, sexy, smart Andie Newman.' Her blush deepened as he sounded each adjective. 'People would certainly believe I could be instantly smitten with such a woman,' he said. 'In fact they'd think I was clever getting a ring on your finger so quickly.'

That flustered her. 'Th...thank you. I... I'm flattered. But it wouldn't seem authentic. We'd have to pretend so much. It would be such deception.'

With any other woman, he'd be waiting for her to ask: *What's in it for me?* Not Andie. He doubted the thought of a reward for her participation had even entered her head. He would have to entice her with an offer she couldn't refuse. And save the big gun to sway her from her final refusal.

'So you're going to say "yes"?'

She shook her head vehemently. 'No. I'm not. It wouldn't be right.'

'What's the harm? You'd be helping me out.'

She spun on her heel away from him and he faced her back view, her tensely hunched shoulders, for a long moment before she turned back to confront him. 'Can't you see it makes a mockery of... of a man and a woman committing to each other? To spending their lives together in a loving union? That's what getting engaged is all about. Not sealing a business deal.'

He closed his eyes at the emotion in her voice, the blurring of her words with choking pain. Under his breath he cursed fluently. Because, from any moral point of view, she was absolutely right.

'Were you engaged to...to Anthony?' he asked.

Her eyes when she lifted them to him glistened with the sheen of unshed tears. 'Not officially. But we had our future planned, even the names of our kids chosen. That's why I know promising to marry someone isn't something you do lightly. And not... not for a scam. Do you understand?'

Of course he did. He'd once been idealistic about love and marriage and sharing his life with that one special woman. But he couldn't admit it. Or that he'd become cynical that that kind of love would ever exist for him. Too much rode on this deal. Including his integrity.

'But this isn't really getting engaged,' he said. 'It's just...a limited agreement.'

Slowly she shook her head. 'I can't help you,' she said. 'Sorry.'

Dominic braced himself. He'd had to be ruthless at times to get where he'd got. To overcome the disadvantages of his youth. *To win.*

'What if by agreeing to be my fake fiancée you were helping someone else?' he said.

She frowned. 'Like who? Helping Walter Burton to make even more billions? I honestly can't say I like the sound of that guy, linking business to people's private lives. He sounds like a hypocrite, for one thing—you know, rich men and eyes of needles and all that. I'm not lying for him.'

'Not Walter Burton. I mean your nephew Timothy.' The little boy was his big gun.

'What do you mean, Timothy?'

Dominic fired his shot. 'Agree to be my fake fiancée and I will pay for all of Timothy's medical treatment—both immediate and ongoing. No limits. Hannah tells me there's a clinic in the United States that's at the forefront of research into treatment for his condition.'

Andie stared at him. 'You've spoken to Hannah? You've told Hannah about this? That you'll pay for Timothy if I agree to—'

He put up his hand. 'Not true.'

'But you—'

'I met with Hannah the day after the dinner with your family to talk about her helping me recruit the families for the party. At that meeting—out of interest—I asked her to tell me more about Timothy. She told me about the American treatment. I offered *then* to pay all the treatment—airfares and accommodation included.'

The colour rushed back into Andie's cheeks. 'That…that was extraordinarily generous of you. What did Hannah say?'

'She refused.'

'Of course she would. She hardly knows you. A Newman wouldn't accept charity. Although I might have tried to convince her.'

'Maybe you could convince her now. If Hannah thought I was going to be part of the family—her brother-in-law, in fact—she could hardly refuse to accept, could she? And isn't it the sooner the better for Timothy's treatment?'

Andie stared at Dominic for a very long moment, too shocked to speak. 'Th…that's coercion. Coercion of the most insidious kind,' she finally managed to choke out.

A whole lot more words she couldn't express also tumbled around in her brain. Ruthless. Conniving. Heartless. And yet…he'd offered to help Timothy well before the fake fiancée thing. *Not a Scrooge after all.* She'd thought she'd been getting to know him—but Dominic Hunt was more of a mystery to her than ever.

He drew his dark brows together. 'Coercion? I wouldn't go that far. But I did offer to help Timothy without any strings attached. Hannah refused. This way, she might accept. And your nephew will get the help he needs. I see it as a win-win scenario.'

Andie realised she was twisting the leather thronging that laced together the front of her top and stopped it. Nothing in her life had equipped her to make this kind of decision. 'You're really putting me on the spot here. Asking me to lie and be someone I'm not—'

'Someone you're not? How does that work? You'd still be Andie.'

She found it difficult to meet his direct, confronting gaze. Those observant grey eyes seemed to see more than she wanted him to. 'You're asking me to pretend to be...to pretend to be a woman in love. When...when I'm not.' She'd only ever been in love once—and she didn't want to trawl back in her memories to try and relive that feeling— love lost hurt way too much. She did have feelings for Dominic beyond the employer/contractor relationship—but they were more of the other 'l' word—lust rather than love.

His eyes seemed to darken. 'I suppose I am.'

'And you too,' she said. 'You would have to pretend to be in love with...with me. And it would have to look darn authentic to be convincing.'

This was why she was prevaricating. As soon as he'd mentioned Timothy, she knew she would have little choice but to agree. If it had been any other blackmailing billionaire she would probably have said "yes" straight away—living a lie for a month would be worth it for Timothy to get the treatment her family's combined resources couldn't afford.

But not *this* man. How could she blithely *pretend* to be in love with a man she wanted as much as she wanted him? It would be some kind of torture.

'I see,' he said. Had he seriously not thought this through?

'We would be playing with big emotions, here, Dominic. And other people would be affected too. My family thinks you hung the moon. They'd be delighted if we dated—a sudden engagement would both shock and worry them. At some stage I would have to introduce you to Anthony's parents—they would be happy for me and want to meet you.'

'I see where you're going,' he said, raking his hand through his hair once more in a gesture that was becoming familiar.

She narrowed her eyes. 'And yet...would it all be worth it for Hannah to accept your help for Timothy?' She put up her hand to stop him from replying. 'I'm thinking out loud here.'

'And helping me achieve something I really want.'

There must be something more behind his drive to get this American deal. She hoped she'd discover it one day, sooner rather than later. It might help her understand him.

'You've backed me into a corner here, Dominic, and I can't say I appreciate it. How can I say "no" to such an incredible opportunity for Timothy?'

'Does that mean your answer is "yes"?'

She tilted her chin upwards—determined not to capitulate too readily to something about which she still had serious doubts. 'That's an unusual way to put it, Dominic—rather like you've made me a genuine proposal.'

Dominic pulled a face but it didn't dull the glint of triumph in his eyes. He thought he'd won. But she was determined to get something out of this deal for herself too.

Andie had no doubt if she asked for recompense—money, gifts—he'd give it to her. Dominic was getting what he wanted. Timothy would be getting what he so desperately needed. But what about *her*?

She wasn't interested in jewellery or fancy shopping. What she wanted was *him*. She wanted to kiss him, she wanted to hold him and she very much wanted to make love with him. Not for fake—for real.

There was a very good chance this arrangement would end in tears—her tears. But if she agreed to a fake engagement with this man, who attracted her like no other, she wanted what a fiancée might be expected to have—*him*. She thought, with a little shiver of desire, about what he'd said: *pleasure all the way.* She would be fine with that.

'Would it help if I made it sound like a genuine proposal?' he said, obviously bemused.

That hurt. Because the way he spoke made it sound as if there was no way he would ever make a genuine proposal to her. Not that she wanted that—heck, she hardly knew the guy. But it put her on warning. *Let's be honest,* she thought. She wanted him in her bed. But she also wanted to make darn sure she didn't get hurt. This was just a business deal to him—nothing personal involved.

'Do it,' she said, pointing to the floor. 'The full down-on-bended-knee thing.'

'Seriously?' he said, dark brows raised.

'Yes,' she said imperiously.

He grinned. 'Okay.'

The tall, black denim-clad hunk obediently knelt down on one knee, took her left hand in both of his and looked up into her face. 'Andie, will you do me the honour of becoming my fake fiancée?' he intoned in that deep, so-sexy voice.

Looking down at his roughly handsome face, Andie didn't know whether to laugh or cry. 'Yes, I accept your proposal,' she said in a voice that wasn't quite steady.

Dominic squeezed her hand hard as relief flooded

his face. He got up from bended knee and for a moment she thought he might kiss her.

'But there are conditions,' she said, pulling away and letting go of his hand.

CHAPTER NINE

Andie almost laughed out loud at Dominic's perplexed expression. He was most likely used to calling the shots—in both business and his relationships. 'Conditions?' he asked.

'Yes, conditions,' she said firmly. 'Come on over to the sofa and I'll run through the list with you. I need to sit down; these heels aren't good for pacing in.' The polished concrete floor was all about looks rather than comfort.

'Do I have any choice about these "conditions"?' he grumbled.

'I think you'll see the sense in them,' she said. This was not going to go all his way. There was danger in this game she'd been coerced into playing and she wanted to make sure she and her loved ones were not going to get hurt by it.

She led him over to the red leather modular sofa in the living area. The apartment in an old converted factory warehouse was owned by one of her roommates and had been furnished stylishly with Andie's help. She flopped down on the sofa, kicked off the leopard stilettos that landed in an animal print clash on the zebra-patterned floor rug, and patted the seat next to her.

As Dominic sat down, his muscular thighs brushed against hers and she caught her breath until he settled at a not-quite-touching distance from her, his arm resting on the back of the sofa behind her. She had to close her eyes momentarily to deal with the rush of awareness from his already familiar scent, the sheer maleness of him in such close proximity.

'I'm interested to hear what you say,' he said, angling his powerful body towards her. He must work out a lot to have a chest like that. She couldn't help but wonder what it would feel like to splay her hands against those hard muscles, to press her body against his.

But it appeared he was having no such sensual thoughts about *her*. She noticed he gave a surreptitious glance to his watch.

'Hey, no continually checking on the clock,' she said. 'You have to give time to an engagement. Especially a make-believe one, if we're to make it believable. Not to mention your fake fiancée just might feel a tad insulted.'

She made her voice light but she meant every word of it. She had agreed to play her role in this charade and was now committed to making it work.

FREE Merchandise is 'in the Cards' for you!

Dear Reader,

We're giving away FREE MERCHANDISE!

Seriously, we'd like to reward you for reading this novel by giving you **FREE MERCHANDISE** worth over $20. And no purchase is necessary!

You see the Jack of Hearts sticker above? Paste that sticker in the box on the Free Merchandise Voucher inside. Return the Voucher promptly...and we'll send you valuable Free Merchandise!

Thanks again for reading one of our novels—and enjoy your Free Merchandise with our compliments!

Pam Powers

Pam Powers

P.S. Look inside to see what Free Merchandise is **"in the cards"** for you!

We'd like to send you two free books like the one you are enjoying now. Your two books have a combined price of over $10, but they are yours to keep absolutely FREE! We'll even send you 2 wonderful surprise gifts. You can't lose!

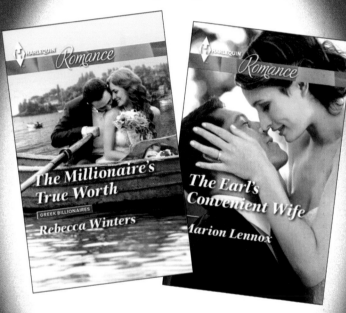

YOUR FREE MERCHANDISE INCLUDES...

2 FREE Books **AND** 2 FREE Mystery Gifts

FREE MERCHANDISE VOUCHER

2 FREE
BOOKS
and
2 FREE
GIFTS

Please send my Free Merchandise, consisting of
2 Free Books and **2 Free Mystery Gifts**.
I understand that I am under no obligation to buy
anything, as explained on the back of this card.

119/319 HDL GH95

Please Print

FIRST NAME

LAST NAME

ADDRESS

APT.#   CITY

STATE/PROV.   ZIP/POSTAL CODE

NO PURCHASE NECESSARY!

HR-N15-FM15

READER SERVICE—Here's how it works:

Accepting your 2 free Harlequin® Romance Larger Print books and 2 free gifts (gifts valued at approximately $10.00) places you under no obligation to buy anything. You may keep the books and gifts and return the shipping statement marked "cancel." If you do not cancel, about a month later we'll send you 4 additional books and bill you just $5.09 each in the U.S. or $5.49 each in Canada. That is a savings of at least 15% off the cover price. It's quite a bargain! Shipping and handling is just 50¢ per book in the U.S. and 75¢ per book in Canada.* You may cancel at any time, but if you choose to continue, every month we'll send you 4 more books, which you may either purchase at the discount price or return to us and cancel your subscription. *Terms and prices subject to change without notice. Prices do not include applicable taxes. Sales tax applicable in N.Y. Canadian residents will be charged applicable taxes. Offer not valid in Quebec. Books received may not be as shown. All orders subject to approval. Credit or debit balances in a customer's account(s) may be offset by any other outstanding balance owed by or to the customer. Please allow 4 to 6 weeks for delivery. Offer available while quantities last.

▲ If offer card is missing write to: Reader Service, P.O. Box 1867, Buffalo, NY 14240-1867 or visit www.ReaderService.com ▲

BUSINESS REPLY MAIL

FIRST-CLASS MAIL   PERMIT NO. 717   BUFFALO, NY

POSTAGE WILL BE PAID BY ADDRESSEE

READER SERVICE
PO BOX 1867
BUFFALO NY 14240-9952

NO POSTAGE
NECESSARY
IF MAILED
IN THE
UNITED STATES

'Fair enough,' he said with a lazy half-smile. 'Is that one of your conditions?'

'Not one on its own as such, but it will fit into the others.'

'Okay, hit me with the conditions.' He feinted a boxer's defence that made her smile.

'Condition Number One,' she said, holding up the index finger of her left hand. 'Hannah never knows the truth—not now, not ever—that our engagement is a sham,' she said. 'In fact, none of my family is *ever* to know the truth.'

'Good strategy,' said Dominic. 'In fact, I'd extend that. *No one* should ever know. Both business partners and friends.'

'Agreed,' she said. It would be difficult to go through with this without confiding in a friend but it had to be that way. *No one must know how deeply attracted she was to him.* She didn't want anyone's pity when she and Dominic went their separate ways.

'Otherwise, the fallout from people discovering they'd been deceived could be considerable,' he said. 'What's next?'

She held up her middle finger. 'Condition Number Two—a plausible story. We need to explain why we got engaged so quickly. So start thinking…'

'Couldn't we just have fallen for each other straight away?'

Andie was taken aback. She hadn't expected

anything that romantic from Dominic Hunt. 'You mean like "love at first sight"?'

'Exactly.'

'Would that be believable?'

He shook his head in mock indignation. 'Again you continue to insult me…'

'I didn't mean…' She'd certainly felt *something* for him at first sight. Sitting next to him on this sofa, she was feeling it all over again. But it wasn't *love*—she knew only too well what it was like to love. To love and to lose the man she loved in such a cruel way. Truth be told, she wasn't sure she wanted to love again. It hurt too much to lose that love.

'I don't like the lying aspect of this any more than you do,' he said. He removed his arm from the back of the sofa so he could lean closer to her, both hands resting on his knees. 'Why not stick to the truth as much as possible? You came to organise my party. I was instantly smitten, wooed you and won you.'

'And I was a complete walkover,' she said dryly.

'So we change it—you made me work very hard to win you.'

'In two weeks—and you away for one of them?' she said. 'Good in principle. But we might have to fudge the timeline a little.'

'It can happen,' he said. 'Love at first sight, I mean. My parents…apparently they fell for each other on day one and were married within mere months of meeting. Or so my aunt told me.'

His eyes darkened and she remembered he'd only been eleven years old when left an orphan. If she'd lost her parents at that age, her world would have collapsed around her—as no doubt his had. But he was obviously trying to revive a happy memory of his parents.

'How lovely—a real-life romance. Did they meet in Australia or England?'

'London. They were both schoolteachers; my mother was living in England. She came to his school as a temporary mathematics teacher; he taught chemistry.'

Andie decided not to risk a feeble joke about their meeting being explosive. Not when the parents' love story had ended in tragedy. 'No wonder you're clever then, with such smart parents.'

'Yes,' he said, making the word sound like an end-of-story punctuation mark. She knew only too well what it was like not to want to pursue a conversation about a lost loved one.

'So we have a precedent for love at first sight in your family,' she said. 'I... I fell for Anthony straight away too. So for both of us an...an instant attraction—if not *love*—could be feasible.' Instant and ongoing for her—but he was not to know that.

That Dominic had talked about his parents surprised her. For her, thinking about Anthony—as always—brought a tug of pain to her heart but this time also a reminder of the insincerity of this venture with Dominic. She knew what real commitment should feel like. But for Timothy to get that vital treatment she was prepared to compromise on her principles.

'Love at first sight it is,' he said.

'*Attraction* at first sight,' she corrected him.

'Surely it would had to have led to love for us to get engaged,' he said.

'True,' she conceded. He tossed around concepts of love and commitment as if they were concepts with which to barter, not deep, abiding emotions between two people who cared enough about each other to pledge a lifetime together. *Till death us do part.* She could never think of that part of a marriage ceremony without breaking down. She shouldn't be thinking of it now.

'Next condition?' he said.

She skipped her ring finger, which she had trouble keeping upright, and went straight for her pinkie. 'Condition Number Three: no dating other people—for the duration of the engagement, that is.'

'I'm on board with that one,' he said without hesitation.

'Me too,' she said. She hadn't even thought about any man but Dominic since the moment she'd met him, so that was not likely to be a hardship.

He sat here next to her in jeans and T-shirt like

a regular thirty-two-year-old guy—not a secretive billionaire who had involved her in a scheme to deceive family and friends to help him make even more money. If he were just your everyday handsome hunk she would make her interest in him known. But her attraction went beyond his good looks and muscles to the complex man she sensed below his confident exterior. She had seen only intriguing hints of those hidden depths—she wanted to discover more.

Andie's thumb went up next. 'Resolution Number Four: I dump you, not the other way around. When this comes to an end, that is.'

'Agreed—and I'll be a gentleman about it. But I ask you not to sell your story. I don't want to wake up one morning to the headline *"My Six Weeks with Scrooge".*'

He could actually *joke* about being a Scrooge— Dominic had come a long way.

'Of course,' she said. 'I promise not to say *"I Hopped Out of the Billionaire's Bed"* either. Seriously, I would never talk to the media. You can be reassured of that.'

'No tacky headlines, just a simple civilised break-up to be handled by you,' he said.

They both fell silent for a moment. Did he feel stricken by the same melancholy she did at the thought of the imagined break-up of a fake engagement? And she couldn't help thinking she'd like a chance to hop *into* his bed before she hopped *out* of it.

'On to Condition Number Five,' she said, holding up all five fingers as she could not make her ring finger stand on its own. 'We have to get to know each other. So we don't get caught out on stuff we would be expected to know about each other if we were truly...committing to a life together.'

How different this fake relationship would be to a real relationship—getting to know each other over shared experiences, shared laughter, shared tears, long lazy mornings in bed...

Dominic sank down further into the sofa, his broad shoulders hunched inward. 'Yup.' It was more a grunt than a word.

'You don't sound keen to converse?'

'What sort of things?' he said with obvious reluctance. Not for the first time, she had a sense of secrets deeply held.

'For one thing, I need to know more about your marriage and how it ended.' And more about his time on the streets. And about that broken nose and scarred knuckles. And why he had let people believe he was a Scrooge when he so obviously wasn't. Strictly speaking, she probably didn't *need* to know all that about him for a fake engagement. Fact was, she *wanted* to know it.

'I guess I can talk to you about my marriage,' he said, still not sounding convinced. 'But there are things about my life that I would rather remain private.'

What things? 'Just so long as I'm not made a fool of at some stage down the track by not knowing something a real fiancée would have known.'

'Fine,' he grunted in a response that didn't give her much confidence. She ached to know more about him. And yet there was that shadow she sensed. She wouldn't push for simple curiosity's sake.

'As far as I'm concerned, my life's pretty much an open book,' she said, in an effort to encourage him to open up about his life—or past, to be more specific. 'Just ask what you need to know about me and I'll do my best to answer honestly.'

Was any person's life truly an open book? Like anyone else, she had doubts and anxieties and dumb things she'd done that she'd regretted, but nothing lurked that she thought could hinder an engagement. No one would criticise her for finding love again after five years. In truth, she knew they would be glad for her. So would Anthony.

She remembered one day, lying together on the beach. *'I would die if I lost you,'* she'd said to Anthony.

'Don't say that,' he'd said. *'If anything happened to me, I'd want you to find another guy. But why are we talking like this? We're both going to live until we're a hundred.'*

'Why not schedule in a question-and-answer session?' Dominic said.

She pulled her thoughts back to the present. 'Good idea,' she said. 'Excellent idea, in fact.'

Dominic rolled his eyes in response.

'Oh,' she said. 'You weren't serious. I… I was.'

'No, you're right. I guess there's no room for spontaneity in a fake engagement.' It was a wonder he could get the words out when his tongue was so firmly in his cheek. 'A question-and-answer session it is. At a time to be determined.'

'Good idea,' she said, feeling disconcerted. Was all this just a game to him?

'Are there any more conditions to come?' he asked. 'You're all out of fingers on one hand, by the way.'

'There is one more very important condition to come—and may I remind you I do have ten fingers—but first I want to hear if there's anything you want to add.'

She actually had two more conditions, but the final condition she could not share with him: *that she could not fall for him*. She couldn't deal with the fallout in terms of pain if she were foolish enough to let down the guard on her heart.

Andie's beautiful green eyes had sparkled with good humour in spite of the awkward position he had put her into. *Coerced* her into. But now her eyes seemed to dim and Dominic wondered if she was being completely honest about being an 'open book'.

Ironically, he already knew more about Andie, the fake fiancée, than he'd known about Tara when he'd got engaged to her for real. His ex-wife had kept her true nature under wraps until well after she'd got the wedding band on her finger. *What you see is what you get.* He so wanted to believe that about Andie.

'My condition? You have to wear a ring,' he said. 'I want to get you an engagement ring straight away. Today. Once Tara sees that she'll know it's serious. And the press will too. Not to mention a symbol for when we meet with Walter Burton.'

She shrugged. 'Okay, you get me a ring.'

'You don't want to choose it yourself?' He was taken aback. Tara had been so avaricious about jewellery.

'No. I would find it…sad. Distressing. The day I choose my engagement ring is the day I get engaged for real. To me, the ring should be a symbol of a true commitment, not a…a prop for a charade. But I agree—I should wear one as a visible sign of commitment.'

'I'll organise it then,' he said. He had no idea why he should be disappointed at her lack of enthusiasm. She was absolutely right—the ring would be a prop. But it would also play a role in keeping it believable. 'What size ring do you wear?'

'I haven't a clue,' she said. She held up her right hand to show the collection of tiny fine silver rings on her slender fingers. Her nails were painted cream today. 'I bought these at a market and just tried them on until I found rings that fitted.' She slid off the ring from the third finger of her right hand. 'This should do the trick.' She handed it to him. It was still warm with her body heat and he held it on his palm for a moment before pocketing it.

'What style of engagement ring would you like?' he asked.

Again she shrugged. 'You choose. It's honestly not important to me.'

A hefty carat solitaire diamond would be appropriate—one that would give her a good resale value when she went to sell it after this was all over.

'Did you choose your ex-wife's engagement ring?' Andie asked.

He scowled at the reminder that he had once got engaged for real.

Andie pulled one of her endearing faces. 'Sorry. I guess that's a sensitive issue. I know we'll come to all that in our question-and-answer session. I'm just curious.'

'She chose it herself. All I had to do was pay

for it.' That alone should have alerted him to what the marriage was all about—giving her access to his money and the lifestyle it bought.

'That wasn't very…romantic,' Andie said.

'There was nothing romantic about my marriage. Shall I tell you about it now and get all that out of the way?'

'If you feel comfortable with it,' she said.

'Comfortable is never a word I would relate to that time of my life,' he said. 'It was a series of mistakes.'

'If you're ready to tell me, I'm ready to listen.' He thought about how Andie had read his mood so accurately earlier this morning—giving him breakfast when he hadn't even been aware himself that he was hungry. She was thoughtful. And kind. Kindness wasn't an attribute he had much encountered in the women he had met.

'The first mistake I made with Tara was that she reminded me of someone else—a girl I'd met when I was living in the squat. Someone frail and sweet with similar colouring—someone I'd wanted to care for and look after.' It still hurt to think of Melody. Andie didn't need to know about her.

'And the second mistake?' Andie asked, seeming to understand he didn't want to speak further about Melody. She leaned forward as if she didn't want to miss a word.

'I believed her when she said she wanted children.'

'You wanted children?'

'As soon as possible. Tara said she did too.'

Andie frowned. 'But she didn't?'

Even now, bitterness rose in his throat. 'After we'd been married a year and nothing had happened, I suggested we see a doctor. Tara put it off and put it off. I thought it was because she didn't want to admit to failure. It was quite by accident that I discovered all the time I thought we'd been trying to conceive, she'd been on the contraceptive pill.'

Andie screwed up her face in an expression of disbelief and distaste. 'That's unbelievable.'

'When I confronted her, she laughed.' He relived the horror of discovering his ex-wife's treachery and the realisation she didn't have it in her to love. Not him. Certainly not a child. Fortunately, she hadn't been clever enough to understand the sub-clauses in the pre-nuptial agreement and divorce had been relatively straightforward.

'You had a lucky escape,' Andie said.

'That's why I never want to marry again. How could I ever trust another woman after that?'

'I understand you would feel that way,' she said. 'But not every woman would be like her. Me… my sisters, my friends. I don't know anyone who would behave with such dishonesty. Don't write off all women because of one.'

Trouble was, his wealth attracted women like Tara.

He was about to try and explain that to Andie when her phone started to sound out a bar of classical music.

She got up from the sofa and headed for the kitchen countertop to pick it up. 'Gemma,' she mouthed to him. 'I'd better take it.'

He nodded, grateful for the reprieve. Tara's treachery had got him into this fake engagement scenario with Andie, who was being such a good sport about the whole thing. He did not want to waste another word, or indeed thought, on his ex. Again, he thanked whatever providence had sent Andie into his life—Andie who was the opposite of Tara in every way.

He couldn't help but overhear Andie as she chatted to Gemma. 'Yes, yes, I saw it. We were having lunch after the meeting that Friday. Yes, it does look romantic. No, I didn't know anyone took a photo.'

Andie waved him over to her. 'Shall I tell her?' she mouthed.

He gave her the thumbs-up. 'Yes,' he mouthed back as he got up. There was no intention of keeping this 'engagement' secret. He walked over closer to Andie, who was standing there in bare feet, looking more beautiful in jeans than any other woman would look in a ball gown.

'Actually, Gemma, I...haven't been completely honest with you. I...uh...we...well, Dominic and I hit it off from the moment we first saw each other.'

Andie looked to Dominic and he nodded—she was doing well.

She listened to Gemma, then spoke again. 'Yes. We are...romantically involved. In fact...well... we're engaged.' She held the phone out from her ear and even Dominic could hear the excited squeals coming from Gemma.

When the squeals had subsided, Andie spoke again. 'Yes. It is sudden. I know that. But...well... you see I've learned that you have to grab your chance at happiness when you can. I... I've had it snatched away from me before.' She paused as she listened. 'Yes, that's it. I didn't want to wait. Neither did he. Gemma, I'd appreciate it if you didn't tell anyone just yet. Eliza? Well, okay, you can tell Eliza. I'd just like to tell my family first. What was that? Yes, I'll tell him.' She shut down her phone.

'So it's out,' he said.

'Yes,' she said. 'No denying it now.'

'What did Gemma ask you to tell me?'

She looked up at him. 'That she hoped you knew what a lucky guy you are to...to catch me.'

He looked down at her. 'I know very well how

lucky I am. You're wonderful in every way and I appreciate what you're doing to help me.'

For a long moment he looked down into her face—still, serious, even sombre without her usual animated expression. Her eyes were full of something he couldn't put a name to. But not, he hoped, regret.

'Thank you, Andie.'

He stepped closer. For a long moment her gaze met his and held it. He saw wariness but he also saw the stirrings of what he could only read as invitation. To kiss his pretend fiancée would probably be a mistake. But it was a mistake he badly wanted to make.

He lifted his hand to her face, brushed first the smooth skin of her cheek and then the warm softness of her lips with the back of his knuckles. She stilled. Her lips parted under his touch and he could feel the tremor that ran through her body. He dropped his hand to her shoulder, then dipped his head and claimed her mouth in a firm gentle kiss. She murmured her surprise and pleasure as she kissed him back.

CHAPTER TEN

DOMINIC WAS KISSING her and it was more wonderful than Andie ever could have imagined. His firm, sensuous mouth was sure and certain on hers and she welcomed the intimate caress, the nudging of his tongue against the seam of her lips as she opened her mouth to his. His beard growth scratched her face but it was a pleasurable kind of pain. *The man knew how to kiss.*

But as he kissed her and she kissed him back she was shocked by the sudden explosion of chemistry between them that turned something gentle into something urgent and demanding. She wound her arms around his neck to bring him closer in a wild tangle of tongues and lips as she pressed herself against his hard muscular chest. He tasted of coffee and hot male and desire. Passion this instant, this insistent was a surprise.

But it was too soon.

She knew she wanted him. But she hadn't realised until now just how *much* she wanted him.

And how careful she would have to be to guard her heart. Because these thrilling kisses told her that intimate contact with Dominic Hunt might just become an addiction she would find very difficult to live without. To him, this pretend engagement was a business ploy that might also develop into an entertaining game on the side. *She did not want to be a fake fiancée with benefits.*

When it came down to it, while she had dated over the last few years, her only serious relationship had been with a boy who had adored her, and whom she had loved with all her heart. Not a man like Dominic, who had sworn off marriage and viewed commitment so lightly he could pretend to be engaged. Her common sense urged her to stop but her body wanted more, more, more of him.

With a great effort she broke away from the kiss. Her heart was pounding in triple time, her breath coming in painful gasps. She took a deep steadying breath. And then another.

'That…that was a great start on Condition Number Six,' she managed to choke out.

Dominic towered over her; his breath came in ragged gasps. He looked so darkly sensual, her heart seemed to flip right over in her chest. 'What?' he demanded. 'Stopping when we'd just started?'

'No. I… I mean the actual kiss.'

He put his hand on her shoulder, lightly stroking her in a caress that ignited shivers of delight all through her.

'So tell me about your sixth condition,' he said, his deep voice with a broken edge to it as he struggled to control his breathing.

'Condition Number Six is that we…we have to look the part.'

He frowned. 'And that means…?'

'I mean we have to act like a genuine couple. To seem to other people as if we're…we're crazy about each other. Because it would have to be… something very powerful between us for us to get engaged so quickly. In…real life, I mean.'

She found it difficult to meet his eyes. 'I was going to say we needed to get physical. And we just did…get physical. So we…uh…know that there's chemistry between us. And that…that it works.'

He dropped his hand from her shoulder to tilt her chin upwards with his finger so she was forced to meet his gaze. 'There was never any doubt about that.'

His words thrummed through her body. That sexual attraction had been there for her the first time she'd met him. *Had he felt it too?*

'So the sixth condition is somewhat superfluous,' she said, her voice racing as she tried to ignore the hunger for him his kiss had ignited. 'I think we might be okay, there. You know, holding hands, arms around each other. Appropriate Public Displays of Affection.' It was an effort to force herself to sound matter of fact.

'This just got to be my favourite of all your conditions,' he said slowly, his eyes narrowing in a way she found incredibly sexy. 'Shall we practise some more?'

Her traitorous body wrestled down her hopelessly outmatched common sense. 'Why not?' she murmured, desperate to be in his arms again. He pulled her close and their body contact made her aware he wanted her as much as she wanted him. She sighed as she pressed her mouth to his.

Then her phone sang out its ringtone of a piano sonata.

'Leave it,' growled Dominic.

She ignored the musical tone until it stopped. But it had brought her back to reality. There was nothing she wanted more than to take Dominic by the hand and lead him up the stairs to her bedroom. She intended to have him before this contract between them came to an end.

But that intuition she usually trusted screamed at her that to make love with him on the first day of their fake engagement would be a mistake. It would change the dynamic of their relationship to something she did not feel confident of being able to handle.

No sooner had the ringtone stopped than it started again.

Andie untangled herself from Dominic's embrace and stepped right back from him, back from the seductive reach of his muscular arms.

'I… I have to take this,' she said.

She answered the phone but had to rest against the kitchen countertop to support knees that had gone shaky and weak. Dominic leaned back against the wall opposite her and crossed his arms against his powerful chest. His muscles flexed as he did so and she had to force herself to concentrate on the phone call.

'Yes, Eliza, it's true. I know—it must have been a surprise to you. A party?' Andie looked up to Dominic and shook her head. He nodded. She spoke to Eliza. 'No. We don't want an engagement party. Yes, I know we're party queens and it's what we do.' She rolled her eyes at Dominic and, to her relief, he smiled. 'The Christmas party is more than enough to handle at the moment,' she said to Eliza.

We. She and Dominic were a couple now. A fake couple. It would take some getting used to. So would handling the physical attraction between them.

'The wedding?' Eliza's question about the timing of the wedding flustered her. 'We…we…uh… next year some time. Yes, I know next year is only next month. The wedding won't be next month, that's for sure.' *The* wedding—wouldn't a loved-up fiancée have said *our* wedding?

She finished the call to Eliza and realised her hands were clammy. 'This is not going to be easy,' she said to Dominic.

'I never thought it would be,' he said. Was there a double meaning there?

'I have no experience in this kind of deception. The first thing Eliza asked me was when are we getting married. She put me on the spot. I... I struggled to find an answer.'

He nodded slowly. 'I suggest we say we've decided on a long engagement. That we're committed but want to use the engagement time to get to know each other better.'

'That sounds good,' she said.

The deceptive words came so easily to him while she was so flustered she could scarcely think. She realised how hopelessly mismatched they were: he was more experienced, wealthier, from a completely different background. And so willing to lie.

And yet... That kiss had only confirmed how much she wanted him.

Her phone rang out again. 'Why do I get the feeling this phone will go all day long?' she said, a note of irritation underscoring her voice. She looked on the caller ID. 'It's my fashion editor friend, Karen. I knew Gemma wouldn't be able to stop at Eliza,' she told Dominic as she answered it.

The first part of the conversation was pretty much a repeat of the conversation she'd had with Gemma. But then Karen asked should she start scouting around for her wedding dress. Karen hunted down bargain-priced clothes for her; of course she'd want to help her with a wedding. 'My wedding dress? We…uh…haven't set a date for the wedding yet. Yes, I suppose it's never too early to think about the dress. Simple? Vintage inspired? Gorgeous shoes?' She laughed and hoped Karen didn't pick up on the shrill edge to her laughter. 'You know my taste only too well, Karen. A veil? A modest lace veil? Okay. Yes. I'll leave it to you. Thank you.'

'Your friends move fast,' Dominic said when she'd disconnected the call.

'They're so thrilled for me. After…after…well, you know. My past.' Her past of genuine love, unsullied by lies and deception.

'Of course,' he said.

She couldn't bring herself to say anything about the kisses they'd shared. It wasn't the kind of thing she found easy to talk about. Neither, it appeared, did he.

He glanced down at his watch. The action drew her attention to his hands. She noticed again how attractive they were, with long strong fingers. And thought how she would like to feel them on her body. Stroking. Caressing. Exploring. *She had to stop this.*

'I know I'm breaking the terms of one of your conditions,' he said. 'But I do have to get to the office. There are cancelled meetings in other states to reschedule and staff who need to talk to me.'

'And I've got to finalise the furniture hire for the Christmas party. With two hundred people for lunch, we need more tables and chairs. It's sobering, to have all those families in need on Christmas Day.'

'Hannah assures me it's the tip of a tragic iceberg,' said Dominic.

They both paused for a long moment before she spoke. 'I also have to work on a tiaras-and-tuxedos-themed twenty-first party. Ironic, isn't it, after what we've just been saying?' But organising parties was her job and brought not only employment to her and her partners but also the caterers, the waiting staff and everyone else involved.

'I didn't think twenty-first parties were important any more, with eighteen the legal age of adulthood,' Dominic said.

'They're still very popular. This lovely girl turning twenty-one still lives at home with her parents and has three more years of university still ahead of her to become a veterinarian. I have to organise tiaras for her dogs.'

'Wh…what?' he spluttered. 'Did you say you're putting a tiara on a *dog*?'

'Her dogs are very important to her; they'll be honoured guests at the party.'

He scowled. 'I like dogs but that's ridiculous.'

'We're getting more and more bookings for dog parties. A doggy birthday boy or girl invites their doggy friends. They're quite a thing. And getting as competitive as the kids' parties. Of course it's a learning curve for a party planner—considering doggy bathroom habits, for one thing.'

'That is the stupidest—'

Andie put up her hand. 'Don't be too quick to judge. The doggy parties are really about making the humans happy—I doubt the dogs could care less. Frivolity can be fun. Eliza and I have laid bets on how many boys will arrive wearing tiaras to the vet student's twenty-first.'

She had to smile at his bah-humbug expression.

'By the time I was twenty-one, I had established a career in real estate and had my first million in sight.'

That interested her. 'I'd love to know about—'

He cut her off. 'Let's save that for the question-and-answer session, shall we?'

'Which will start…?'

'This afternoon. Can you come to my place?'

'Sure. It doesn't hurt to visit the party site as many times as I can.'

'Only this time you'll be coming to collect your engagement ring.'

'Of…of course.' She had forgotten about that. In a way, she dreaded it. 'And to find out more about you, fake fiancé. We have to be really well briefed to face my family tomorrow evening.'

She and Anthony had joked that by the time they'd paid off their student loans all they'd be able to afford for an engagement ring would be a ring pull from a can of soft drink. The ring pull would have had so much more meaning than this cynical exercise.

She felt suddenly subdued at the thought of deceiving her family. Her friends were used to the ups and downs of dating. A few weeks down the track, they'd take a broken engagement in their stride. If those kisses were anything to go by, she might be more than a tad upset when her time with Dominic came to an end. She pummelled back down to somewhere deep inside her the shred of hope that perhaps something real could happen between them after the engagement charade was done.

'When will you tell your parents?' Dominic asked.

'Today. They'd be hurt beyond belief if they found out from someone else.'

'And you'll talk to Hannah about Timothy?'

'At the family dinner. We should speak to her and Paul together.'

'I hope she won't be too difficult to convince. I really want to help that little boy.'

'I know,' she said, thinking of how grateful her family would be to him. How glad she was she'd agreed to all this for her tiny nephew's sake. But what about Dominic's family? This shouldn't be all about hers. 'What about your aunt? Do we need to tell her?'

The shutters came slamming down. 'No. She's out of the picture.'

The way he said it let her know not to ask more. Not now anyway.

Dominic shrugged on his leather jacket in preparation to go. She stared, dumbstruck, feasting her eyes on him. *He was so hot.* She still felt awkward after their passionate kissing session. Should she reach up and kiss him on the cheek?

While she was making up her mind, he pulled her close for a brief, exciting kiss on her mouth. She doubted there could be any other type of kiss but exciting from Dominic. 'Happy to fulfil Condition Number Six at any time,' he said, very seriously.

She smiled, the tension between them immediately dissipated. But she wasn't ready to say goodbye just yet.

'Before you go...' She picked up her smartphone again. 'The first thing my friends who don't know you will want to see is a photo of my surprise new fiancé.'

He ran his hand over his unshaven chin. 'Like this? Can't it wait?'

'I like your face like that. It's hot. No need to shave on my behalf.' Without thinking, she put her fingers up to her cheek, where there was probably stubble rash. *His kiss had felt so good.*

'If you say so,' he said, looking pleased.

'Just lean against the door there,' she said. 'Look cool.'

He slouched against the door and sent her a smouldering look. The wave of want that crashed through her made her nearly drop the phone. 'Do I look *cool*?' he said in a self-mocking tone. 'I thought you liked *hot*?'

'You know exactly what I mean.' She was discovering a light-hearted side to Dominic she liked very much.

Their gazes met and they both burst into laughter. He looked even more gorgeous when he laughed, perfect teeth white in his tanned face, and she immediately captured a few more images of him. Who would recognise this good-humoured hunk in jeans and leather jacket as the billionaire Scrooge of legend?

'What about a selfie of us together?' she asked. 'In the interests of authenticity,' she hastily added.

Bad idea. She stood next to him, aware of every centimetre of body contact, and held her phone out in front of them. She felt more self-conscious than she could ever remember feeling. He pulled her in so their faces were close together. She smiled and clicked, and as she clicked again he kissed her on the cheek.

'That will be cute,' she said.

'Another?' he asked. This time he kissed her on the mouth. *Click. Click. Click.* And then she forgot to click.

After he had left, Andie spent more minutes than she should scrolling through the photos on her phone. *No one would know they were faking it.*

CHAPTER ELEVEN

DOMINIC NOW KNEW more about diamond engagement rings than even a guy who was genuinely engaged to be married needed to know. He'd thought he could just march into Sydney's most exclusive jewellery store and hand over an investment-sized price for a big chunk of diamond. Not so.

The sales guy—rather, *executive consultant*—who had greeted him and ushered him into a private room had taken the purchase very seriously. He'd hit Dominic with a barrage of questions. It was unfortunate that the lady was unable to be there because it was very important the ring would suit her personality. What were the lady's favourite colours? What style of clothes did she favour? Her colouring?

'Were you able to answer the questions?' Andie asked, her lips curving into her delightful smile.

She had just arrived at his house. After she'd taken some measurements in the old ballroom, he had taken her out to sit in the white Hollywood-style chairs by the pool. Again, she looked as if she belonged. She wore a natural-coloured linen dress with her hair piled up and a scarf twisted and tied right from the base of her neck to the top of her head. It could have looked drab and old-fashioned but, on her, with her vintage sunglasses and orange lipstick, it looked just right.

Last time she'd been there he'd been so caught up with her he hadn't thought to ask her would she like a drink. He didn't want a live-in house-keeper—he valued his privacy too much—but his daily housekeeper had been this morning and the refrigerator was well stocked. He'd carried a se-lection of cool drinks out to the poolside table be-tween their two chairs.

'You're finding this story amusing, aren't you?' he said, picking up his iced tea.

She took off her sunglasses. 'Absolutely. I had no idea the rigmarole involved in buying an en-gagement ring.'

'Me neither. I thought I'd just march in, point out a diamond ring and pay for it.' This was a first for him.

'Me too,' said Andie. 'I thought that's what guys did when they bought a ring.'

'Oh, no. First of all, I'd done completely the wrong thing in not having you with me. He was too discreet to ask where you were, so I didn't have to come up with a creative story to explain your absence.'

'One less lie required anyway,' she said with a twist of her lovely mouth. 'Go on with the story—I'm fascinated.'

'Apparently, the done thing is to have a bespoke ring—like the business suits I have made to measure.'

'A bespoke ring? Who knew?' she said, her eyes dancing.

'Instead, I had to choose from their ready-to-wear couture pieces.'

'I had no idea such a thing existed,' she said with obvious delight. *Her smile.* It made him feel what he'd thought he'd never feel again, made him want what he'd thought he'd never want.

'You should have been there,' he said. 'You would have had fun.' He'd spent the entire time in the jewellery store wishing she'd been by his side. He could imagine her suppressing giggles as the consultant had run through his over-the-top sales pitch.

'Perhaps,' she said, but her eyes dimmed. 'You know my reasons for not wanting to get involved in the purchase. Anyway, what did you tell them about my—' she made quote marks in the air with her fingers '—"personal style"? That must have put you on the spot?'

'I told the consultant about your misbehaving

skirt—only I didn't call it that, of course. I told him about your shoes that laced up your calves. I told him about your turquoise necklace and your outsized earrings. I told him about your leopard-print shoes and your white trousers.'

Andie's eyes widened. 'You remember all that about what I wear?'

'I did say I was observant,' he said.

Ask him to remember what Party Planners Numbers One to Three had been wearing for their interviews and he would scarcely recall it. But he remembered every detail about her since that errant breeze at his front door had blown Andie into his life.

At the jewellery store, once he'd relaxed into the conversation with the consultant, Dominic had also told him how Andie was smart and creative and a touch unconventional and had the most beautiful smile and a husky, engaging laugh. 'This is a lucky lady,' the guy had said. 'You must love her very much.'

That had thrown Dominic. 'Yes,' he'd muttered. *Love* could not enter into this. He did not want Andie to get hurt. And hurt wasn't on his personal agenda either. He didn't think he had it in him to love. To give love you had to be loved—and genuine love was not something that had been part of his life.

'So… I'm curious,' said Andie. What kind of ring did you—did I—end up with?'

'Not the classic solitaire I would have chosen. The guy said you'd find it boring.'

'Of course I wouldn't have found it boring,' she said not very convincingly.

'Why do I not believe you?' he said.

'Stop teasing me and show me the darn ring,' she said.

Dominic took out the small, leather, case from his inside suit jacket pocket. 'I hope you like it,' he said. *He wanted her to like it.* He didn't know why it was suddenly so important that she did.

He opened the case and held it out for Andie to see. Her eyes widened and she caught her breath. 'It…it's exquisite,' she said.

'Is it something you think you could wear?' he asked.

'Oh, yes,' she said. 'I love it.'

'It's called a halo set ring,' he said. 'The ring of little diamonds that surround the big central diamond is the halo. And the very narrow split band—again set with small diamonds—is apparently very fashionable.'

'That diamond is enormous,' she said, drawing back. 'I'd be nervous to wear it.'

'I got it well insured,' he said.

'Good,' she said. 'If I lost it, I'd be paying you

back for the rest of my life and probably still be in debt.'

'The ring is yours, Andie.'

'I know, for the duration,' she said. 'I promise to look after it.' She crossed her heart.

'You misunderstand. The ring is yours to keep after…after all this has come to an end.'

She frowned and shook her head vehemently. 'No. That wasn't part of the deal. Timothy's treatment was the deal. I give this ring back to you when…when I dump you.'

'We'll see about that,' he said, not wanting to get into an argument with her. As far as he was concerned, this ring was *hers*. She could keep it or sell it or give it away—he never wanted it back. 'Now, shouldn't I be getting that diamond on your finger?'

He was surprised to find his hand wasn't steady as he took the ring out of its hinged case. It glittered and sparkled as the afternoon sunlight danced off the multi-cut facets of the diamonds. 'Hold out your hand,' he said.

'No', she said, again shaking her head. 'Give it to me and I'll put it on myself. This isn't a real engagement and I don't want to jinx myself. When I get engaged for real, my real fiancé will put my ring on my wedding finger.'

Again, Dominic felt disappointed. Against all reason. He wanted to put the ring on her finger.

But he understood why he shouldn't. He felt a pang of regret that he most likely would never again be anyone's 'real fiancé'—and a pang of what he recognised as envy for the man who would win Andie's heart for real.

He put the ring back in its case. 'You do want to get married one day?'

He wasn't sure if she was still in love with the memory of her first boyfriend—and that no man would be able to live up to that frozen-in-time ideal. Melody had been his first love—but he certainly held no romanticised memories of her.

'Of course I do. I want to get married and have a family. I... I... It took me a long time to get over the loss of my dreams of a life with Anthony. I couldn't see myself with anyone but him. But that was five years ago. Now... I think I'm ready to move on.'

Dominic had to clear his throat to speak. 'Okay, I see your point. Better put on the ring yourself,' he said.

Tentatively, she lifted the ring from where it nestled in the velvet lining of its case. 'I'm terrified I'll drop it and it will fall into the pool.' She laughed nervously as she slid it on to the third finger of her left hand. 'There—it's on.' She held out her hand, fingers splayed to better display the ring. 'It's a perfect fit,' she said. 'You did well.'

'It looks good on you,' he said.

'That sales guy knew his stuff,' she said. 'I can't stop looking at it. It's the most beautiful ring I've ever seen.' She looked up at him. 'I still have my doubts about the wisdom of this charade. But I will enjoy wearing this magnificent piece of jewellery. Thank you for choosing something so perfect.'

'Thank you for helping me out with this crazy scheme,' he said. The scheme that had seemed crazy the moment he'd proposed it and which got crazier and crazier as it went along. But it was important he sealed that deal with Walter Burton. And was it such a bad thing to have to spend so much time with Andie?

Andie took a deep breath to try and clear her head of the conflicting emotions aroused by wearing the exquisite ring that sat so perfectly on her finger. *The ring pull would have been so much more valuable.* This enormous diamond with its many surrounding tiny diamonds symbolised not love and commitment but the you-scratch-my-back-and-I'll-scratch-yours deal between her and Dominic.

Still, she couldn't help wondering how he could have chosen a ring so absolutely *her*.

'I've been thinking about our getting-to-know-each-other session,' she said. 'Why don't we each ask the other three questions?'

'Short and to the point,' he said with obvious relief.

'Or longer, as needs might be. I want to be the best fake fiancée I can. No way do I want to be caught out on something important I should know about you. I didn't like the feeling this morning when I froze as Karen questioned me about our wedding plans.'

Dominic drank from his iced tea. To give himself time to think? Or plan evasive action? 'I see where you're going. Let's see if we can make it work.'

Andie settled back in the chair. She didn't know whether to be disappointed or relieved there was a small table between her and Dominic. She would not be averse to his thigh nudged against hers—at the same time, it would undoubtedly be distracting. 'Okay. I'll start. My Question Number One is: How did you get from street kid to billionaire?'

Dominic took his time to put his glass back down on the table. 'Before I reply, let's get one thing straight.' His gaze was direct. 'My answers are for you and you alone. What I tell you is to go no further.'

'Agreed,' she said, meeting his gaze full-on. 'Can we get another thing straight? You can trust me.'

'Just so long as we know where we stand.'

'I'm surprised you're not making me sign a contract.' She said the words half in jest but the expression that flashed across his face in response made her pause. She sat forward in her seat. 'You thought about a contract, didn't you?'

With Dominic back in his immaculate dark business suit, clean-shaven, hair perfectly groomed, she didn't feel as confident with him as she had this morning.

'I did think of a contract and quickly dismissed it,' he said. 'I do trust you, Andie.'

Surely he must be aware that she would not jeopardise Timothy's treatment in any way? 'I'm glad to hear that, Dominic, because this won't work if we don't trust each other—it goes both ways. Let's start. C'mon—answer my question.'

He still didn't answer. She waited, aware of the palm leaves above rustling in the same slight breeze that ruffled the aquamarine surface of the pool, the distant barking of a neighbour's dog.

'You know I hate this?' he said finally.

'I kind of get that,' she said. 'But I couldn't "marry" a man whose past remained a dark secret to me.'

Even after the question-and-answer session, she suspected big chunks of his past might remain a secret from her. Maybe from anyone.

He dragged in a deep breath as if to prepare himself for something unpleasant. 'As I have already mentioned, at age seventeen, I was homeless. I was living in an underground car park on the site of an abandoned shopping centre project in one of the roughest areas of Brisbane. The buildings had only got to the foundation stage. The car park was…well, you can imagine what an underground car park that had never been completed was like. It was a labyrinth of unfinished service areas and elevator shafts. No lights, pools of water whenever it rained, riddled with rats and cockroaches.'

'And human vermin too, I'll bet.' Andie shuddered. 'What a scary place for a teenager to be living—and dangerous.'

He had come from such a dark place. She could gush with sympathy and pity. But she knew instinctively that was not what he wanted to hear. Show how deeply moved she was at the thought of seventeen-year-old Dominic living such a perilous life and he would clam up. And she wanted to hear more.

Dominic's eyes assumed a dark, faraway look as though he was going back somewhere in his mind he had no desire to revisit. 'It was dangerous and smelly and seemed like hell. But it was also somewhere safer to sleep than on the actual streets. Darkness meant shadows you could hide in, and feel safe even if it was only an illusion of safety.'

She reached out and took the glass from his

hand; he seemed unaware he was gripping it so tightly he might break it. 'Your home life must have been kind of hellish too for you to have preferred that over living with your aunt.'

'Hell? You could say that.' The grim set of his mouth let her know that no more would be forthcoming on that subject.

'Your life on the streets must have been…terrifying.'

'I toughened up pretty quick. One thing I had in my favour was I was big—the same height I am now and strong from playing football at school. It was a rough-around-the-edges kind of school, and I'd had my share of sorting out bullies there.' He raised his fists into a fighting position in a gesture she thought was unconscious.

So scratch the elite private school. She realised now that Dominic was a self-made man. And his story of triumph over adversity fascinated her. 'So you could defend yourself against thugs and…and predators.'

Her heart went out to him. At seventeen she'd had all the security of a loving family and comfortable home. But she knew first-hand from her foster sisters that not all young people were that fortunate. It seemed that the young Dominic had started off with loving parents and a secure life but had spiralled downwards from then on. What the heck was wrong with the aunt to have let that happen?

She reached over the table and trailed her fingers across his scarred knuckles. 'That's how you got these?' It was amazing the familiarity a fake engagement allowed.

'I got in a lot of fights,' he said.

'And this?' She traced the fine scar at the side of his mouth.

'Another fight,' he said.

She dropped her hands to her sides, again overwhelmed by that urge to comfort him. 'You were angry and frightened.'

He shifted uncomfortably in his seat. 'All that.'

'But then you ended up with this.' She waved her hand to encompass the immaculate art deco pool, the expensively landscaped gardens, the superb house. It was an oasis of beauty and luxury.

'My fighting brought me to the attention of the police. I was charged with assault,' he said bluntly.

She'd thought his tough exterior was for real—had sensed the undercurrents of suppressed rage.

'Believe me, the other guy deserved it,' he said with an expression of grim satisfaction. 'He was drug-dealing scum.'

'What happened? With the police, I mean.' He'd been seventeen—still a kid. All she'd been fighting at that age was schoolgirl drama.

'I got lucky. The first piece of luck was that I

was under eighteen and not charged as an adult. The second piece of luck was I was referred to a government social worker—Jim, his name was. Poor man, having to deal with the sullen, unhappy kid I was then couldn't have been easy. Jim was truly one of the good guys—still is. He won my confidence and got me away from that squat, to the guidance of another social worker friend of his down the Queensland Gold Coast.'

'Sun, surf and sand,' she said. She knew it sounded flippant but Dominic would not want her to pity his young self.

'And a booming real estate market. The social worker down there was a good guy too. He got me a job as a gofer in a real estate agency. I was paid a pittance but it was a start and I liked it there. To cut a long story short, I was soon promoted to the sales team. I discovered I was good at selling the lifestyle dream, not just the number of bedrooms and bathrooms. I became adept at gauging what was important to the client.'

'Because you were observant,' she said. And tough and resilient and utterly admirable.

'That's important. Especially when I realised the role the woman played in a residential sale. Win her over and you more than likely closed the sale.'

Andie could see how those good looks, along with intuition and charm and the toughness to back it up, could have accelerated him ahead. 'Fascinating. And incredible how you've kept all the details away from the public. Surely people must have tried to research you, would have wanted to know your story?'

'As a juvenile, my record is sealed. I've never spoken about it. It's a time of my life I want well behind me. Without Jim the social worker, I might have gone the other way.'

'You mean you could have ended up as a violent thug or a drug dealer? I don't believe that for a second.'

He shrugged those broad street-fighter shoulders. 'I appreciate your faith in me. But, like so many of my fellow runaways, I could so easily have ended up…broken.'

Andie struggled to find an answer to that. 'It… it's a testament to your strength of character that you didn't.'

'If you say,' he said. But he looked pleased. 'Once I'd made enough money to have my own place and a car—nowhere as good as your hatchback, I might add—I started university part-time. I got lucky again.'

'You passed with honours?' She hadn't seen a university degree anywhere in her research on him but there was no harm in asking.

'No. I soon realised I knew more about making money and how business operated than some of the teachers in my commerce degree. I dropped out after eighteen months. But in a statistics class I met Jake Marlow. He was a brilliant, misunderstood geek. Socially, I still considered myself an outcast. We became friends.'

'And business partners, you said.' He was four years older than she was, and yet had lived a lifetime more. And had overcome terrible odds to get where he had.

'He was playing with the concept of groundbreaking online business software tools but no bank would loan him the money to develop them. I was riding high on commissions. We set up a partnership. I put in the money he needed. I could smell my first million.'

'Let me guess—it was an amazing success?'

'That software is used by thousands of businesses around the world to manage their digital workflow. We made a lot of money very quickly. Jake is still developing successful new software.' His obvious pride in his friend warmed his words.

'And you're still business partners.'

He nodded. 'The success of our venture gave me the investment dollars I needed to also spin off into my own separate business developing undervalued homemaker centres. We call them bulky goods centres—furnishing, white goods, electricals.'

'I guess the Gold Coast got too small for you.' That part she'd been able to research.

'I moved to Sydney. You know the rest.'

In silence she drank her mineral water with lime, he finished his iced tea. He'd given her a lot to think about. Was that anger that had driven him resolved? Or could it still be bubbling under the surface, ready to erupt?

He angled himself to look more directly at her. 'Now it's your turn to answer my question, Andie,' he said. 'How did you get over the death of your... of Anthony?'

She hadn't been expecting that and it hit her hard. But he'd dug deep. She had to too. 'I... I don't know that I will ever be able to forget the shock of it. One minute he was there, the next minute gone. I... I was as good as a widow, before I'd had the chance to be a bride.'

Dominic nodded, as if he understood. Of course he'd lost his parents.

'We were staying the weekend at his parents' beach house at Whale Beach. Ant got up very early, left a note to say he'd gone surfing, kissed me—I was asleep but awake enough to know he was going out—and then he was gone. Of course I blamed myself for not going with him. Then I was angry he'd gone out by himself.'

'Understandably,' he said and she thought again how he seemed to see more than other people. She had no deep, dark secrets. But, if she did, she felt

he'd burrow down to them without her even re-
alising it.

'After Anthony died, I became terrified of the
sea. I hated the waves—blamed them for taking
him from me, which I know was all kinds of irrational. Then one day I went to the beach by myself
and sat on the sand. I remember hugging my knees
as I watched a teenage boy, tall and blond like Anthony, ride a wave all the way into the shore, saw
the exultation on his face, the sheer joy he felt at
being one with the wave.'

'If this is bringing back hurtful memories, you
don't have to go any further.'

'I'm okay... When someone close dies, you look
for a sign from them—I learned I wasn't alone in
that when I had counselling. That boy on his board
was like a message from Anthony. He died doing
something he truly loved. I ran into the surf and
felt somehow connected to him. It was a healing
experience, a turning point in my recovery from
grief.'

'That's a powerful story,' Dominic said.

'The point of it is, it's five years since he died
and of course I've moved on. Anyone who might
wonder if my past could affect our fake future can
be assured of that. Anthony was part of my youth;
we grew up together. In some ways I'm the person
I am because of those happy years behind me. But

I want happy years ahead of me too. I've dated. I just haven't met the right person.'

For the first time she wondered if she could feel more for Dominic than physical attraction. For a boy who had been through what he had and yet come through as the kind of man who offered to pay for a little boy's medical treatment? Who was more willing to open his house to disadvantaged people than celebrities? There was so much more to Dominic than she ever could have imagined—and the more she found out about him the more she liked about him.

And then there were those kisses she had not been able to stop thinking about—and yearning for more.

'I appreciate you telling me,' he said.

She poured herself another long, cool mineral water. Offered to pour one for Dominic, but he declined.

'On to my next question,' she said. 'It's about your family. Do you have family other than your aunt? My mother will certainly want to know because she's already writing the guest list for the wedding.'

'You told your mother about the engagement?'

'She couldn't be more delighted. In fact…well… she got quite tearful.' Andie had never felt more hypocritical than the moment she realised her mother was crying tears of joy for her.

'That's a relief,' he said.

'You could put it that way. I didn't realise quite how concerned they were about me being…lonely. Not that I am lonely, by the way—I have really good friends.' But it was not the same as having a special someone.

'I'm beginning to see that,' he said. 'I'm surprised we've been able to have this long a conversation without your phone going off.'

'That's because I switched it off,' she said. 'There'll probably be a million messages when I switch it back on.'

'So your mother didn't question our…haste?'

'No. And any guilt I felt about pulling the wool over her eyes I forced firmly to the back of my mind. Timothy getting the treatment he needs is way more important to my family than me finding a man.' She looked at him. 'So now—the guest list, your family?'

'My aunt and my mother were the only family each other had. So there is no Australian family.'

'Your aunt has…has passed away?' There was something awkward here that she didn't feel comfortable probing. But they were—supposedly—planning to get married. It made sense for her to know something of his family.

'She's in the best of residential care, paid for by me. That's all I want to say about her.'

'Okay,' she said, shaken by the closed look on his face.

'I have family in the UK but no one close since my grandparents died.'

'So no guests from your side of the family for our imaginary wedding?'

'That's right. And I consider the subject closed. In fact, I've had a gutful of talking about this stuff.'

'Me too,' she said. Hearing about his difficult youth, remembering her early loss was making her feel down. 'I reckon we know enough about each other now to be able to field any questions that are thrown at us. After all, we're not pretending to have known each other for long.'

She got up from her chair, walked to the edge of the pool, knelt at the edge and swished her hand through the water. 'This is such a nice pool. Do you use it much?'

'Most days I swim,' he said, standing behind her. 'There's a gym at the back of the cabana too.'

She imagined him working out in his gym, then plunging into the pool, muscles pumped, spearing through the water in not many clothes, maybe in *no* clothes.

Stop it!

She got up, wishing she could dive in right now to cool herself down. 'Do you like my idea to hire some lifeguards so the guests can swim on Christmas Day?'

'It's a good one.'

'And you're okay with putting a new swimsuit and towel in each of the children's goody bags? Hannah pointed out that some of the kids might not have a swimsuit.'

'I meant to talk to you about that,' he said. Surely he wasn't going to query the cost of the kids' gifts? She would be intensely disappointed if he did. 'I want to buy each of the adults a new swimsuit too; they might not have one either,' he said. 'I don't want anyone feeling excluded for any reason we can avoid.'

She looked up at him. 'You're not really a Scrooge, are you?'

'No,' he said.

'I don't think people are going to be calling you that for much longer. Certainly not if I've got anything to do with it.'

'But not a word about my past.'

'That's understood,' she said, making a my-lips-are-sealed zipping motion over her mouth. 'Though I think you might find people would admire you for having overcome it.'

The alarm on her watch buzzed. 'I'm running late,' she said. 'I didn't realise we'd been talking for so long.'

'You have an appointment? I was going to suggest dinner.'

'No can do, I'm afraid.' Her first impulse was

to cancel her plans, to jump at the opportunity to be with Dominic. But she would not put her life on hold for the fake engagement.

'I have a hot date with a group of girlfriends. It's our first Tuesday of the month movie club. We see a movie and then go to dinner. We're supposed to discuss the movie but we mainly catch up on the gossip.' She held out her hand, where the diamond flashed on the third finger of her left hand. 'I suspect this baby is going to be the main topic of conversation.'

She made to go but, before she could, Dominic had pulled her close for a kiss that left not a scrap of lipstick on her mouth and her hair falling out of its knot.

It was the kind of kiss she could get used to.

CHAPTER TWELVE

ANDIE SAT AT her desk in the Party Queens' head-quarters. 'Headquarters' was rather a grand term for their premises. It comprised an industrial kitchen where Gemma could do her thing; a work-room used for making props; a storage area; and an area loosely termed an office, where she and her two partners squeezed in their desks.

To say they were frantically busy would be an understatement. The weeks leading up to Christmas and New Year were the busiest time of the year for established party planners. For a new company like Party Queens to be so busy was gratifying. But it was the months after the end of the long Aussie summer vacation they had to worry about for advance bookings. Business brain, Eliza, was very good at reminding them of that.

Andie's top priority was Dominic's Christmas party. Actually, it was no longer just his party. As his fiancée, she had officially become co-host. But that didn't mean she wasn't flat-out with other bookings, including a Christmas Eve party for the parents of their first eighteenth party girl. Andie wanted to pull out all the stops for the people who'd given Party Queens their very first job. And then there was the business of being Dominic's fake fiancée—almost a job on its own.

Andie had been 'engaged' to Dominic for ten days and so far so good. She'd been amazed that no one had seriously queried the speed at which she had met, fallen in love with and agreed to marry a man she had known for less than a month.

The swooning sighs of 'love at first sight' and 'how romantic' from her girlfriends she understood, not so much the delight from her pragmatic father and the tears of joy from her mother. She hardly knew Dominic and yet they were prepared to believe she would commit her life to him?

Of course it was because her family and friends had been worried about her, wanted her to be happy, had been concerned she had grieved for Anthony for too long.

'Your dad and I are pleased for you, sweetheart, we really are,' her mother had said. 'We were worried you were so fearful about loving someone again in case you lost them, that you wouldn't let yourself fall in love again,' she'd continued. 'But Dominic is so strong, so right for you; I guess he just broke through those barriers you'd spent so long putting up. And I understand you didn't want to waste time when you knew what it was like to have a future snatched away from you.'

Really? She'd put up *barriers*? She'd just been trying to find someone worthy of stepping into Anthony's shoes. Now she'd found a man who had big boots of his own and would never walk in another man's shadow. *But he wasn't really hers.*

'You put us off the scent by telling us Dominic wasn't your type,' Gemma had said accusingly. Gemma, who was already showing her ideas for a fabulous wedding cake she planned to bake and decorate for her when the time came. Andie felt bad going through images of multi-tiered pastel creations with Gemma, knowing the cake was never going to happen.

Condition Number One, that she and Dominic didn't *ever* tell *anyone* about the deception, seemed now like a very good idea. To hear that their engagement had been a cold-blooded business arrangement was never going to go down well with all these people wishing them well.

At last Wednesday's family dinner, Dominic had been joyfully welcomed into the Newman family. 'I'm glad you saw sense about how hot he was,' her sister Bea had said, hugging her. 'And as for that amazing rock on your finger... Does Dominic have a brother? No? Well, can you find me someone just like him, please?'

But every bit of deception was all worth it for

Timothy. After the family dinner, Andie and Dominic had drawn Hannah and Paul aside. Now that Dominic was to be part of the family—or so they thought—her sister and her husband didn't take much convincing to accept Dominic's offer of paying all Timothy's medical expenses.

Dominic's only condition was that they kept him posted on their tiny son's progress. 'Of course we will,' Hannah had said, 'but Andie will keep you updated and you'll see Timothy at family functions. You'll always be an important part of his life.' And the little boy had more chance of a better life, thanks to Dominic's generosity.

Later, Hannah had hugged her sister tight. 'You've got yourself a good man, Andie, a very, very good man.'

'I know,' said Andie, choked up and cringing inside. She was going to have to come up with an excellent reason to explain why she 'dumped' Dominic when his need for the fake engagement was over.

There had only been one awkward moment at the dinner. Her parents wanted to put an announcement of the engagement in the newspaper. 'Old-fashioned, I know, but it's the right thing to do,' her mother had said.

She'd then wanted to know what Dominic's middle name was for the announcement. Appar-

ently full names were required, Andrea Jane Newman was engaged to Dominic *who*?

She had looked at Dominic, eyes widened by
panic. She should have known that detail about the
man she was supposedly going to marry.

Dominic had quickly stepped in. 'I've kept quiet
about my middle name because I don't like it very
much,' he'd said. 'It's Hugo. Dominic Hugo Hunt.'

Of course everyone had greeted that announcement with cries of how much they loved the name
Hugo. 'You could call your first son Hugo,' Bea
had suggested.

That was when Andie had decided it was time
to go home. She felt so low at deceiving everyone,
she felt she could slink out of the house at ankle
level. If it wasn't for Timothy, she would slide that
outsize diamond off her finger and put an end to
this whole deception.

Dominic had laughed the baby comment off—
and made no further mention of it. He'd wanted
a baby with his first wife—how did he feel about
children now?

Her family was now expecting babies from her
and Dominic. She had not anticipated having to
handle that expectation. But of course, since then,
the image of a dear little boy with black spiky hair
and grey eyes kept popping into her mind. A little
boy who would be fiercely loved and never have
to face the hardships his father had endured.

She banished the bordering on insane thoughts to the area of her brain reserved for impossible dreams. Instead, she concentrated on confirming the delivery date of two hundred and ten—the ten for contingencies—small red-and-white-striped hand-knitted Christmas stockings for Dominic's party. They would sit in the centre of each place setting and contain all the cutlery required by that person for the meal.

She had decided on a simple red-and-white theme, aimed squarely at pleasing children as well as the inner child of the adults. Tables would be set up in the ballroom for a sit-down meal served from a buffet. She wanted it to be as magical and memorable as a Christmas lunch in the home of a billionaire should be—but without being intimidating.

Gemma had planned fabulous cakes, shaped and frosted like an outsize white candle and actually containing a tea light, to be the centrepiece of each table. Whimsical Santa-themed cupcakes would sit at each place with the name of the guest piped on the top. There would be glass bowls of candy canes and masses of Australian Christmas bush with its tiny red flowers as well as bowls of fat red cherries.

Andie would have loved to handle all the decorations herself but it was too big a job. She'd hired one of her favourite stylists to coordinate all the decorations. Jeremy was highly creative and she trusted his skills implicitly. And, importantly, he'd been happy to work on Christmas Day.

She'd been careful not to discuss anything too 'Christmassy' with Dominic, aware of his feelings about the festive season. He still hadn't shared with her just why he hated it so much; she wondered if he ever would. There was some deep pain there, going right back to his childhood, she suspected.

The alarm on her computer flashed a warning at her the same time the alarm on her watch buzzed. Not that she needed any prompts to alert her that she was seeing Dominic this evening.

He had been in meetings with Walter Burton all afternoon. Andie was to join them for dinner. At her suggestion, the meal was to be at Dominic's house. Andie felt that a man like Walter might prefer to experience home-style hospitality; he must be sick of hotels and restaurants. Not that Dominic's house was exactly the epitome of cosy, but it was elegant and beautiful and completely lacking in any brash, vulgar display of wealth.

A table set on the terrace at the front of the house facing the harbour. A chef to prepare the meal. A skilled waiter to serve them. All organised by Party Queens with a menu devised by Gemma. Eliza had, as a matter of course, checked with Walter's personal assistant as to the tycoon's personal dietary requirements.

Then there would be Andie, on her best fiancée behaviour. After all, Mr Burton's preference for doing business with a married man was the reason behind the fake engagement.

Not that she had any problem pretending to be an attentive fiancée. That part of the role came only too easily. Her heartbeat accelerated just at the thought of seeing Dominic this evening. He'd been away in different states on business and she'd only seen him a few times since the family dinner. She checked her watch again. There was plenty of time to get home to Newtown and then over to Vaucluse before the guest of honour arrived.

Dominic had been in Queensland on business and only flown back into Sydney last night. He'd met Walter Burton from a very early flight from the US this morning. After an afternoon of satisfactory meetings, Dominic had taken him back to his hotel. The American businessman would then make his own way to Vaucluse for the crucial dinner with Dominic and Andie.

As soon as he let himself in through the front door of the house Dominic sensed a difference. There was a subtle air of expectation, of warmth. The chef and his assistant were in the kitchen and, if enticing aromas had anything to do with it, dinner was under way. Arrangements of exotic orchids were discreetly arranged throughout the house. That was thanks to Andie.

It was all thanks to Andie. He would have felt uncomfortable hosting Walter Burton in his house if it weren't for her. He would have taken him to an upscale restaurant, which would have been nice but not the same. The older man had been very pleased at the thought of being invited to Dominic's home.

And now here she was, heading towards him from the terrace at the eastern end of the house where they would dine. He caught his breath at how beautiful she looked in a body-hugging cream top and matching long skirt that wrapped across the front and revealed, as she walked, tantalising glimpses of long slender legs and high heeled ankle-strap sandals. Her hair was up, but tousled strands fell around her face. Her only jewellery was her engagement ring. With her simple elegance, again she looked as if she belonged in this house.

'You're home,' she said in that husky voice, already so familiar.

Home. That was the difference in his house this evening. *Andie's presence made it a home.* And he had not felt he'd had a real home for a long time.

But Andie and her team were temporary hired help—she the lead actress in a play put on for the benefit of a visiting businessman. *This was all just for show.*

Because of Walter Burton, because there were strangers in the house, they had to play their roles—he the doting fiancé and she his betrothed.

Andie came close, smiling, raised her face for his kiss. Was that too for show? Or because she was genuinely glad to see him? At the touch of her lips, hunger for her instantly ignited. He closed his eyes as he breathed in her sweet, spicy scent, not wanting to let her go.

A waiter passed by on his way to the outdoor terrace, with a tray of wine glasses.

'I've missed you,' Andie murmured. For the waiter's benefit or for Dominic's? She sounded convincing but he couldn't be sure.

'Me too—missed you, I mean,' he said stiffly, self-consciously.

That was the trouble with this deception he had initiated. It was only too easy to get caught between a false intimacy and an intimacy that could possibly be real. Or could it? He broke away from her, stepped back.

'Is this another misbehaving skirt?' he asked.

He resisted the urge to run his hand over the curve of her hip. It would be an appropriate action for a fiancé but stepping over the boundaries of his agreement with Andie. Kisses were okay—their public displays of affection had to look authentic.

Caresses of a more intimate nature, on the other hand, were *not* okay.

She laughed. 'No breeze tonight so we'll never know.' She lowered her voice. 'Is there anything else you need to brief me about before Mr Burton arrives? I've read through the background information you gave me. I think I'm up to speed on what a fiancée interested in her future husband's work would most likely know.'

'Good,' he said. 'I have every faith you won't let me down. If you're not sure of anything, just keep quiet and I'll cover for you. Not that I think I'll have to do that.'

'Fingers crossed I do you proud,' she said.

Walter Burton arrived punctually—Dominic would have been surprised if he hadn't. The more time he spent with his prospective joint venture partner, the more impressed he was by his acumen and professionalism. *He really wanted this deal.*

Andie greeted the older man with warmth and charm. Straight away he could see Walter was impressed.

She led him to the front terrace where the elegantly set round table—the right size for a friendly yet business orientated meal—had been placed against a backdrop of Sydney Harbour, sparkling blue in the light of the long summer evening. As they edged towards the longest day on December the twenty-second, it did not get dark until after nine p.m.

Christmas should be cold and dark and frosty. He pushed the painful thought away. Dwelling on the past was not appropriate here, not when an important deal hung in the balance.

Andie was immediately taken with Walter Burton. In his mid-sixties and of chunky build, his silver hair and close-trimmed silver beard gave him an avuncular appearance. His pale blue eyes actually sparkled and she had to keep reminding herself that he could not be as genial as he appeared and be such a successful tycoon.

But his attitude to philanthropy was the reason she was here, organising the party, pretending to be Dominic's betrothed. He espoused the view that making as much money as you could was a fine aim—so long as you remembered to share it with those who had less. 'It's a social responsibility,' he said.

Dominic had done nothing but agree with him. There was not a trace of Scrooge in anything he said. Andie had begun to believe the tag was purely a media invention.

Walter—he insisted she drop the 'Mr Burton'—seemed genuinely keen to hear all the details of the Christmas party. He was particularly interested when she told him Dominic had actively sought to dampen press interest. That had, as intended, flamed media interest. They already had two journalists volunteer to help out on that day—quite an achievement considering most people wanted to spend it with their families or close friends.

Several times during the meal, Andie squeezed Dominic's hand under the table—as a private signal that she thought the evening was going well. His smile in return let her know he thought so too. The fiancée fraud appeared to be doing the trick.

The waiter had just cleared the main course when Walter sat back in his chair, relaxed, well fed and praising the excellent food. Andie felt she and Dominic could also finally relax from the knife-edge of tension required to impress the American without revealing the truth of their relationship.

So Walter's next conversational gambit seemed to come from out of the blue. 'Of course you understand the plight of your Christmas Day guests, Dominic, as you've come from Struggle Street yourself,' he said. 'Yet you do your utmost to hide it.'

Dominic seemed shocked into silence. Andie watched in alarm as he blanched under his tan and gripped the edge of the table so his knuckles showed white. 'I'm not sure what you mean,' he said at last.

Walter's shrewd eyes narrowed. 'You've covered your tracks well, but I have a policy of never doing business with someone I haven't fully researched. I know about young Nick Hunt and the trouble he got into.'

Dominic seemed to go even paler. 'You mean the assault charge? Even though it never went to court. Even though I was a juvenile and there should be no record of it. How did you—?'

'Never mind how I found out. But I also discovered how much Dominic Hunt has given back to the world in which he had to fight to survive.' Walter looked to Andie. 'I guess you don't know about this, my dear.'

'Dominic has told me about his past,' she said cautiously. She sat at the edge of her seat, feeling trapped by uncertainty, terrified of saying the wrong thing, not wanting to reveal her ignorance of anything important. 'I also know how very generous he is.'

'Generous to the point that he funds a centre to help troubled young people in Brisbane.' Andie couldn't help a gasp of surprise that revealed her total lack of knowledge. 'He hasn't told you about his Underground Help Centre?' Walter didn't wait for her to answer. 'It provides safe emergency accommodation, health care, counselling, rehab—all funded by your fiancé. Altogether a most admirable venture.'

Why had Dominic let everyone think he was a Scrooge?

'You've done your research well, Walter,' Dominic said. 'Yes, I haven't yet told Andie about the centre. I wanted to take her to Brisbane and show her the work we do there.'

'I'll look forward to that, darling,' she said, not having to fake her admiration for him.

Dominic addressed both her and Walter. 'When I started to make serious money, I bought the abandoned shopping centre site where I'd sought refuge as a troubled runaway and redeveloped it. But part of the site was always going to be for the Underground Help Centre that I founded. I recruited Jim, the social worker who had helped me, to head it up for me.'

Andie felt she would burst with pride in him. Pride and something even more heartfelt. He must hate having to reveal himself like this.

Walter leaned towards Dominic. 'You're a self-made man and I admire that,' he said. 'You're sharing the wealth you acquired by your own hard work and initiative and I admire that too. What I don't understand, Dominic, is why you keep all this such a big secret. There's nothing to be ashamed of in having pulled yourself up by your bootstraps.'

'I'm not ashamed of anything I've done,' Dominic said. 'But I didn't want my past to affect my future success. Especially, I didn't want it to rub off on my business partner, Jake Marlow.'

Andie felt as if she was floundering. Dominic

had briefed her on business aspects she might be expected to know about tonight, but nothing about this. She could only do what she felt was right. Without hesitation, she reached out and took his hand so they stood united.

'People can be very judgemental,' she said to Walter. 'And the media seem to be particularly unfair to Dominic. I'm incredibly proud of him and support his reasons for wanting to keep what he does in Brisbane private. To talk about that terrible time is to relive it, over and over again. From what Dominic has told me, living it once would be more than enough for anyone.'

Dominic squeezed her hand back, hard, and his eyes were warm with gratitude. Gratitude and perhaps—just perhaps—something more? 'I can't stop the nightmares of being back there,' he said. 'But I can avoid talking about it and bringing those times back to life.'

Andie angled herself to face Walter full-on. She was finding it difficult to keep her voice steady. 'If people knew about the centre they'd find out about his living rough and the assault charge. People who don't know him might judge him unfairly. At the same time, I'd love more people to know how generous and kind he actually is and—' She'd probably said enough.

Walter chuckled. 'Another thing he's done right is his choice of fiancée.'

Dominic reached over to kiss her lightly on the lips. 'I concur, Walter,' he said. Was it part of the act or did he really mean it?

'Th…thank you,' stuttered Andie. She added Walter to the list of people who would be disappointed when she dumped Dominic.

'I'm afraid I can't say the same for your choice of first wife,' Walter said.

Dominic visibly tensed. 'What do you mean?'

'I met with her and your former employee this morning. He's an impressive guy, though not someone I feel I want to do business with. But your ex-wife made it clear she would do anything—and I stress *anything*—to seal the deal. She suggested that to me—happily married for more than forty years and who has never even looked at another woman.'

Dominic made a sound of utter disgust but nothing more. Andie thought more of him that he didn't say anything to disparage Tara, appalling though her behaviour had been. Dominic had more dignity.

'The upshot of this is, Dominic, that you are exactly the kind of guy I want to do business with. You and your delightful wife-to-be. You make a great team.'

Dominic reached over to take Andie's hand again. 'Thank you, Walter. Thank you from us both.'

Andie smiled with lips that were aching from

all her false smiles and nodded her thanks. The fake engagement had done exactly what it was intended to. She should be jubilant for Dominic's sake. But that also meant there would soon be no need to carry on with it. And that made her feel miserable. *She wasn't doing a very good job of guarding her heart.*

When Andie said goodnight to Dominic, she clung to him for a moment longer than was necessary. Playing wife-to-be for the evening had made her start to wish a real relationship with Dominic could perhaps one day be on the cards.

Perhaps it was a good thing she wouldn't see Dominic again until Christmas Eve. He had to fly out to Minneapolis to finalise details with Walter, leaving her to handle the countdown to the Christmas party. And trying not to think too much about what had to happen after Christmas, when her 'engagement' would come to an end.

CHAPTER THIRTEEN

IT WAS MIDDAY on Christmas Eve and as Andie pushed open the door into Dominic's house she felt as if she was stepping into a nightmare. The staircase railings were decorated as elegantly as she'd hoped, with tiny lights and white silk cord. The wreath on the door was superb. But dominating the marble entrance hall was an enormous Christmas tree, beautifully decorated with baubles and ornaments and winking with tiny lights. She stared at it in shocked disbelief. *What the heck was that doing there?*

When she said it out loud she didn't say *heck* and she didn't say it quietly.

Her stylist Jeremy's assistant had been rearranging baubles on the lower branches of the tree. She jumped at Andie's outburst and a silver bauble smashed on to the marble floor. Calmly, very calmly, Andie asked the girl where Jeremy was. The girl scuttled out to get him.

Throughout all the Christmas party arrangements, through all the fake fiancée dramas, Andie had kept her cool. Now she was in serious danger of losing it. She had planned this party in meticulous detail. Of all the things that could go wrong, it would have to be this—Dominic would think she had deliberately defied his specific demand. And she didn't want him thinking badly of her.

Jeremy came into the room with a swathe of wide red ribbons draped over his outstretched arm. Andie recognised them as the ones to be looped and tied into extravagant bows on the back of the two hundred chairs in the ballroom.

She had to grit her teeth to stop herself from exploding. 'Why is there a Christmas tree in here?' Her heart was racing with such panic she had to put her hand on her chest to try and slow it.

'Because this entrance space cried out for one. How can you have a Christmas party without a tree?' Jeremy said. 'I thought you'd made a mistake and left it off the brief. Doesn't it look fabulous?'

'It does indeed look fabulous. Except the client specifically said *no tree*.' She could hear her voice rising and took a deep breath to calm herself.

How had she let this happen? Maybe she should have written *NO CHRISTMAS TREE* in bold capitals on every page of the briefing document. She'd arrived here very early this morning to let the decorating crew in and to receive final deliveries of the extra furniture. Jeremy had assured her that all was on track. And it was—except for this darn tree.

'But why?' asked Jeremy. 'It seems crazy not to have a tree.'

Crazy? Maybe. She had no idea why—because Dominic, for all his talk with Walter Burton over dinner that night that had seemed so genuine, still refused to let her in on the events in his past he held so tightly to himself. He'd drip-fed some of the details but she felt there was something major linked to Christmas he would not share. It made her feel excluded—put firmly in her place as no one important in his life. And she wanted to be important to him. She swallowed hard. *Had she really just admitted that to herself?*

'The client actually has a thing against Christmas trees,' she said. 'You might even call it a phobia. For heaven's sake, Jeremy, why didn't you call me before you put this up?' Her mouth was dry and her hands felt clammy at the thought of Dominic's reaction if he saw the tree.

'I'm sorry,' said Jeremy, crestfallen. 'You didn't specify not to include a tree in the decorations. I was just using my initiative.'

On other jobs she'd worked with Jeremy she'd told him to think for himself and not bother her with constant calls, so she couldn't be *too* cranky with him. Creative people could be tricky to manage—

and Jeremy's work was superb. The tree was, in fact, perfect for the spot where he'd placed it.

She took a step back to fully appraise its impact. The tree looked spectacular, dressed in silver with highlights of red, in keeping with her overall colour scheme. She sighed her pleasure at its magnificence. This perfect tree would make a breathtaking first impression for the guests tomorrow. To the children it would seem to be the entrance to a magical world. It spoke of tradition, of hope, of generosity. Everything they were trying to achieve with this party. It would make Dominic look good.

The beautiful tree was beginning to work its magic on her. Surely it would on Dominic too? He'd come such a long way since that first day, when he'd been so vehemently anti everything Christmas. *Christmas was not Christmas without a tree.*

She took a series of deep, calming breaths. Dominic should at least have the chance to see the tree in place. To see how wonderful it looked there. Maybe the sight of this tree would go some way towards healing those hidden deep wounds he refused to acknowledge.

She turned to Jeremy, the decision firm in her mind. 'We'll leave it. You've done such a good job on the tree, it would be a real shame to have to take it down.'

'What about the client?'

'He's a client but he's also my fiancé.' The lie threatened to choke her but she was getting more adept at spinning falsehoods. 'Leave him to me. In the meantime, let me give you a hand with placing the final few ornaments on the lower branches,' she said. She was wearing work clothes—jeans, sneakers and a loose white shirt. She rolled up her sleeves and picked up an exquisite glass angel. Her hand wasn't quite steady—if only she was as confident as she had tried to appear.

Dominic was due back in to Sydney early this evening. *What if he hated the tree?* Surely he wouldn't. He seemed so happy with everything else she'd done for the party; surely he would fall in love with the tree.

But it would take a Christmas miracle for him to fall in love with *her.*

She longed for that miracle. Because she couldn't deny it to herself any longer—she had developed feelings for him.

Dominic had managed to get an earlier flight out of Minneapolis to connect with a non-stop flight to Sydney from Los Angeles. Nonetheless, it was a total flight of more than twenty hours. Despite the comfort of first class, he was tired and anxious to get away from the snow and ice of Minnesota and home to sunny Sydney. A bitterly cold Christmas wasn't quite as he'd remembered it to be.

Overriding everything else, he wanted to get home to Andie. He had thought about her non-stop the whole trip, wished she'd been with him. Next time, he'd promised Walter, he'd bring Andie with him.

As the car he'd taken from the airport pulled up in front of his house, his spirits lifted at the thought of seeing her. He hadn't been able to get through to her phone, so he'd called Party Queens. Eliza had told him she was actually at his house in Vaucluse, working on the decorations for the party.

On the spur of the moment, he'd decided not to let her know he'd got in early. It might be better to surprise her. He reckoned if she didn't know he was coming, she wouldn't have time to put on her fake fiancée front. Her first reaction to him would give him more of a clue of her real feelings towards him.

Because while he was away he had missed her so intensely, he'd been forced to face *his* real feelings towards *her*. He was falling in love with her. Not only was he falling in love with her; he realised he had never had feelings of such intensity about a woman.

Melody had been his first love—and sweet, damaged Melody had loved him back to the extent she was capable of love. But it hadn't been enough. That assault charge had happened because he had been protecting her. Protecting her from a guy assaulting her in an alley not far from the takeaway food shop where he'd worked in the kitchen in return for food and a few dollars cash in hand.

But the guy had been her dealer—and possibly her pimp. Melody had squealed at Dominic to leave the guy alone. She'd shrieked at him that she knew what she was doing; she didn't need protecting. Dominic had ignored her, had pulled the creep off her, smashed his fist into the guy's face. Then the dealer's mates had shown up and Dominic had copped a beating too. But, although younger than the low-lifes, he'd been bigger, stronger and inflicted more damage. The cops had taken him in, while the others had disappeared into the dark corners that were their natural habitat. And Melody had gone with them without a backward glance, leaving him with a shattered heart as well as a broken nose. He'd never seen her again.

Of course Melody hadn't been her real name. He'd been too naïve to realise that at the time. Later, when he'd set up the Underground Help Centre, he'd tried to find her but without any luck. He liked to think she was living a safe happy life somewhere but the reality was likely to be less cosy than that.

Then there'd been Tara—the next woman to have betrayed him. The least thought he gave to his ex-wife the better.

But Andie. Andie was different. He felt his

heart, frosted over for so long, warm when he thought about her. *What you saw was what you got.* Not only smart and beautiful, but loyal and loving. He'd told her more about his past than he'd ever told anyone. He could be himself with her, not have to pretend, be Nick as well as Dominic. Be not the billionaire but the man. Their relationship could be real. *He could spend his life with Andie.*

And he wanted to tell her just that.

The scent of pine needles assaulted his senses even before he put his key in his front door. The sharp resin smell instantly revived memories of that Christmas Eve when he'd been eleven years old and the happy part of his childhood had come to its terrible end. Christmas trees were the thing he most hated about Christmas.

The smell made him nauseous, started a headache throbbing in his temples. Andie must be using pine in some of the decorations. It would have to go. He couldn't have it in the house.

He pushed the door silently open—only to recoil at what he saw.

There was a Christmas tree in his house. A whopping great Christmas tree, taking up half his entrance hallway and rising high above the banisters of the staircase.

What the hell? He had told Andie in no uncertain terms there was to be no Christmas tree—

anywhere. He gritted his teeth and fisted his hands by his sides. *How could she be so insensitive?*

There was a team of people working on the tree and its myriad glitzy ornaments. Including Andie. He'd never thought she could be complicit in this defiance of his wishes. He felt let down. *Betrayed.*

She turned. Froze. Her eyes widened with shock and alarm when she saw him. A glass ornament slid from her hands and smashed on the floor but she scarcely seemed to notice.

'What part of "no Christmas tree" did you not get, Andie?'

She got up from her kneeling position and took a step towards him, put up her hands as if to ward off his anger. The people she was with scuttled out of the room, leaving them alone. But he bet they were eavesdropping somewhere nearby. The thought made him even more livid.

'Dominic, I'm sorry. I know you said no tree.'

'You're damn right I did.'

'It was a mistake. The tree was never meant to be here. There were some…some crossed lines. I wasn't expecting it either. But then I saw it and it's so beautiful and looks so right here. I thought you might…appreciate it, might see how right it is and want to keep it.'

He could feel the veins standing out on his neck, his hands clenched so tight they hurt. 'I don't see it as beautiful.'

Her face flushed. She would read that as an insult to her skills. He was beyond caring. 'Why? Why do you hate Christmas trees?' she said. 'Why this...this irrational dislike of Christmas?'

Irrational? He gritted his teeth. 'That's none of your concern.'

'But I want it to be. I thought I could help you. I—'

'You thought wrong.'

Now her hands were clenched and she was glaring at him. 'Why won't you share it with me— what makes you hurt so much at this time of year? Why do I have to guess? Why do I have to tiptoe around you?' Her voice rose with each question as it seemed her every frustration and doubt rushed to the surface.

Dominic was furious. How dared she put him through this...this humiliation?

'Don't forget your place,' he said coldly. 'I employ you.' With each word he made a stabbing motion with his finger to emphasise the words. 'Get rid of the tree. Now.'

He hated the stricken look on Andie's face, knowing he had put it there. But if she cared about him at all she never would have allowed that tree to enter his house. He could barely stand to look at her.

For a long moment she didn't say anything. 'Yes,'

she said finally, her voice a dull echo of its usual husky charm. 'Yes, sir,' she added.

In a way he appreciated the defiance of the hissed 'sir'. But he was tired and jet-lagged and grumpy and burning with all the pain and loss he associated with Christmas—and Christmas trees in particular. Above all, he was disappointed in her that she thought so little of his wishes that she would defy him.

His house was festooned with festive paraphernalia. Everywhere he looked, it glittered and shone, mocking him. He'd been talked into this damn party against his wishes. *He hated Christmas.* He uttered a long string of curses worthy of Scrooge.

'I'm going upstairs. Make sure this tree is gone when I come back down. And all your people as well.' He glared in the general direction of the door through which her team had fled.

She met his glare, chin tilted upwards. 'It will take some time to dismantle the tree,' she said. 'But I assure you I will get rid of every last stray needle so you will never know it was there.' She sounded as though she spoke through gritted teeth. 'However, I will need all my crew to help me. We have to be here for at least a few more hours. We still have to finish filling the goody bags and setting the tables.' She glared at him. 'This is *your* party. And you know as well as I do that it must go on. To prove you're not the Scrooge people think you are.'

Some part of him wanted to cross the expanse of floor between them and hug her close. To tell her that of course he understood. That he found it almost impossible to talk about the damage of his childhood. To knuckle down and help her adorn his house for the party tomorrow. But the habits of Christmases past were hard to break.

So was the habit of closing himself off from love. Letting himself love Andie would only end in disappointment and pain, like it had with every other relationship. For her as well as himself. *It seemed he was incapable of love.*

'Text me when you're done,' he said.

He stomped up the stairs to his study. And the bottle of bourbon that waited there.

Andie felt humiliated, angry and upset. How dared Dominic speak to her like that? *'Don't forget your place.'* His harsh words had stabbed into her heart.

Jeremy poked his head around the door that connected through to the living room. She beckoned him to come in. She forced her voice to sound businesslike, refused to let even a hint of a tear burr her tone. 'I told you he wouldn't be happy with the tree.' Her effort at a joke fell very flat.

'Don't worry about it,' Jeremy said, putting a comforting hand on her shoulder. 'We'll get rid of this tree quick-smart. No matter your man is in a mood. The show has to go on. You've got two hundred people here for lunch tomorrow.'

'Thanks, Jeremy,' she said. 'Dominic has just got off a long flight. He's not himself.' But her excuses for him sounded lame even to her own ears.

Was that angry man glaring at her with his fists clenched at his sides the true Dominic? She'd known the anger was there bubbling below the surface, was beginning to understand the reasons for it. But she'd thought that anger that had driven him to violence was in his past. How could she possibly have thought she'd fallen in love with him? She didn't even know the man.

'What do you suggest we do with the tree?' Jeremy asked. 'There are no returns on cut trees.'

Andie's thoughts raced. 'We've got a Christmas Eve party happening elsewhere tonight. The clients have put up a scrappy old artificial tree that looks dreadful. We'll get this delivered to them with the compliments of Party Queens. Keep whatever ornaments you can use here; the rest we'll send with the tree. Let's call a courier truck now.'

Seething, she set to work dismantling the beautiful tree. As she did so, she felt as if she were dismantling all her hopes and dreams for love with Dominic. The diamond ring felt like a heavy burden on her finger, weighted by its duplicity and hypocrisy. While he'd stood there insulting her, she'd felt like taking the ring off and hurling it at him. If it had hit him and drawn blood she would have been glad. His words had been so harsh they felt like they'd drawn blood from her heart.

But of course she couldn't have thrown her ring at him while there were other people in the house. She would be professional right to the end. After all, wasn't she known for her skill at dealing with difficult people?

In spite of that, she'd had her fill of this particular difficult man. He'd got what he wanted from her in terms of his American deal. She'd got what her family needed for Timothy. Both sides of the bargain fulfilled. He'd been her employer, her fake fiancé—she'd liked to think they'd become friends of a sort. She'd wanted more—but that was obviously not to be. She'd stick it out for the Christmas lunch. Then she'd be out of here and out of his life.

The crew worked efficiently and well. When they were done and the tree was gone she waved them goodbye and wished them a Merry Christmas. But not before asking them to please not repeat what they might have heard today. Talk of Dominic's outburst could do serious damage to the rehabilitation of his Scrooge image.

By the time they had all gone it was early evening. She stood and massaged the small of her back where it ached. She would let Dominic know she was done and going home. But she had no intention of texting him as he'd asked. Not asked. *Demanded.* She had things to say that had to be said in person.

CHAPTER FOURTEEN

WITH A HEAVY HEART—wounded hearts *hurt*—
Andie made her way up the stylishly decorated
staircase, its tiny lights discreetly winking. She
hadn't been up here before, as this part of the
house was off-limits for the party. When she
thought of it, she actually had no idea where Dominic could be.

The first two doors opened to two fashionably
furnished empty bedrooms. The third bedroom
was obviously his—a vast bed with immaculate stone-coloured linens, arched windows that
opened to a sweeping view of the harbour. But he
wasn't there.

Then she noticed a door ajar to what seemed
like a study.

There was no response to her knock, so she
pushed it open. The blinds were drawn. Dominic
lay sprawled asleep on a large chesterfield sofa.
The dull light of a tall, arching floor lamp pooled
on him and seemed to put him in the spotlight.

His black lace-up business shoes lay haphazardly at the end of the sofa. He had taken off his jacket and removed his tie. The top buttons of his shirt were undone to reveal an expanse of bare, well-muscled chest her traitorous libido could not help but appreciate as it rose and fell in his sleep.

His right arm fell to the floor near a bottle of bourbon. Andie picked it up. The bottle was nearly full, with probably no more than a glassful gone. Not enough for him to be drunk—more likely collapsed into the sleep of utter exhaustion. She put the bottle on the desk.

There was a swivel-footed captain's chair near the sofa with a padded leather seat. She sat on the edge of it and watched Dominic as he slept. Darn it, but that wounded heart of hers beat faster as she feasted her eyes on his face, which had become so familiar. So...so—she nearly let herself think *so beloved*. But that couldn't be.

She swallowed hard at the lump that rose in her throat. Why on earth had she let herself fall for a man who was so difficult, so damaged, so completely opposite to the man who had made her so happy in the past?

Dominic's hair stood up in spikes. He obviously hadn't shaved since he'd left Minneapolis and his beard was in that stubble stage she found so incredibly sexy. She hadn't realised how long and thick his eyelashes were. His mouth was slightly parted.

She longed to lean over and kiss it. She sighed. There would be no more kissing of this man.

He moaned in his sleep and she could see rapid eye movement behind his lids as if he were being tortured by bad dreams. She could not help but reach out to stroke his furrowed forehead. He returned to more restful sleep. Then his eyes flickered open. Suddenly he sat up, startling her. He looked around, disorientated, eyes glazed with sleep. He focused on her.

'Andie,' he breathed. 'You're here.' He gave a huge sigh, took her hand and kissed it. 'I didn't think I'd ever see you again.'

He didn't deserve to, she thought. But her resolve was weakening.

'Are you okay?' she said, trying to ignore the shivers of pleasure that ran up her arm from his kiss. He had been rude and hurtful to her.

'I've just had a horrible dream,' he said.

'What kind of dream?'

'A nightmare. I was in a cemetery and saw my own headstone.'

She shook her head. 'No, Dominic—I don't want to hear this.' The day of Anthony's funeral had been the worst day of her life. When she'd had to accept she'd never see him again. She couldn't bear to think of Dominic buried under a headstone.

But he continued in a dramatic tone she didn't

think was appropriate for such a gruesome topic. 'It said: 'Here lies Dominic—they called him Scrooge'. And I think it was Christmas Day.'

Not so gruesome after all. She couldn't help a smile.

'You think my nightmare was funny?' he said, affronted.

'I'm sure it was scary at the time. But you'll never be called Scrooge again. Not after tomorrow. I… I'm sorry about what I said earlier. About your…your Scroogeness, I mean.'

He slammed the hand that wasn't holding hers against his forehead. 'The Christmas tree. I'm sorry, Andie. That was unforgivable. Pay your crew a bonus to make up for it, will you, and bill it to me.'

Did he think everything could be solved by throwing money at it?

'I'm also sorry about the tree, Dominic. It was an honest mistake. It's all gone now.'

Maybe she'd been in the wrong too, to imagine he might like the tree when he'd been so vehement about not having one in the house. But she hadn't been wrong about expecting better behaviour from him.

He shuddered. 'It was a shock. The smell of it. The sight of it. Brought back bad memories.'

She shifted in her seat but did not let go of his hand. 'Do you think it might be time to tell me why Christmas trees upset you so much? Because I didn't like seeing that anger. Especially not directed at me. How can I understand you when I don't know what I'm dealing with?'

He grimaced as if stabbed by an unpleasant memory. 'I suppose I have to tell you if I want you to ever talk to me again.'

'I'm talking to you now.'

She remembered what she'd said about recalling unpleasant memories being like reliving them. But this had to come out—one way or another. Better it was with words than fists.

'Christmas Eve is the anniversary of my parents' deaths.'

She squeezed his hand. 'Dominic, I'm so sorry.' That explained a lot. 'Why didn't you say so before?'

'I… I didn't want people feeling sorry for me,' he said gruffly.

'People wouldn't have… Yes, they would have felt sorry for you. But in a good way.' Could all this Scrooge business have been solved by him simply explaining that? 'Can you tell me about it now?'

'There…there's more. It was cold and frosty. My parents went out to pick up the Christmas tree. A deer crossed the road and they braked to avoid it. The road was icy and the car swerved out of control and crashed into a barrier. That's how they died. Getting the damn Christmas tree.'

She couldn't find the words to say anything other than she was sorry again.

'It was…it was my fault they died.'

Andie frowned. 'How could it be your fault? You were eleven years old.'

'My aunt told me repeatedly for the next six years it was my fault.'

'I think you'd better tell me some more about this aunt.'

'The thing is, it really *was* my fault. I'd begged my parents for a real tree. We had a plastic one. My best friend had a real one; I wanted a real one. If they hadn't gone out to get the tree I wanted they wouldn't have died.'

'You've been blaming yourself all these years? It was an accident. How any competent adult could let you blame yourself, I can't imagine.'

'Competent adult and my aunt aren't compatible terms,' he said, the bitterness underlying his words shocking her.

'I keep asking you about her; it's time you gave me some answers.' Though she was beginning to dread what she might hear.

'She used alcohol and prescription meds to mask her serious psychological problems. I know that now as an adult. As a kid, I lived with a bitter woman who swung between abuse and smothering affection.'

'And, as a kid, you put up with a lot in the hope

of love,' Andie said softly, not sure if Dominic actually heard her. She could see the vulnerability in that strong-jawed handsome face, wondered how many people he had ever let be aware of it. She thought again of that little boy with the dark hair. Her vision of Dominic's son merged with that of the young, grieving, abused Dominic. And her heart went out to him.

The words spilled out of him now, words that expressed emotions dammed for years. 'She was particularly bad at Christmas because that's when she'd lost her sister—which was, in her eyes, my fault. When she got fed up with me, she locked me in a cupboard. The physical abuse stopped when I got bigger than her. The mental abuse went on until the day I ran away. Yet all that time she held down a job and presented a reasonable face to the world. I talked to a teacher at school and he didn't believe me. Told me to man up.'

'I honestly don't know what to say...' But she hated his aunt, even though she was aware she'd been a deeply troubled person. No child should be treated like that.

'Say nothing. I don't want to talk about it any more. I'm thirty-two years old. That was all a long time ago.'

'But, deep down, you're still hurting,' she whispered. 'Dominic, I'm so sorry you had to go through all that. And I admire you so much for what you became after such a difficult start.'

Words could only communicate so much. Again, she felt that urge to comfort him. This time, she acted on it. She leaned over to him and kissed him, tasted bourbon on his lips, welcomed the scrape of his stubble on her skin. Immediately, he took the kiss deeper.

The kiss went on and on, passion building, thrilling her. But it was more than sensual pleasure; it was a new sense of connection, of shared emotion as well as sensation.

He broke the kiss to pull her shirt up and over her head. His shirt was already half unbuttoned. It didn't take much to have it completely undone and to slide it off his broad shoulders and muscular arms. She caught her breath in awe at the male perfection of his body.

She wanted him. Dominic had got what he wanted from Walter. Timothy was booked for the treatment he needed. She had promised herself to go after what she wanted—him—and now was her time. It might never be more than this. She knew it and was prepared to take that risk. But she hoped for so much more.

She hadn't known him for long but she had the same kind of certainty—that it could be for ever—as she'd felt for Anthony. A certainty she'd thought she'd never feel again. *For ever love.* Had she been given a chance for that special connection again? She thought *yes*, but could she convince Dominic she could bring him the kind of happiness that had seemed to evade him—that he deserved?

He threw his head back and moaned his pleasure as she planted urgent kisses down the firm column of his throat, then back up to claim his mouth again. He tasted so good, felt so good.

He caught her hands. 'Andie, is this what you want? Because we have to stop it now if you don't,' he said, his voice husky with need.

'Don't you dare stop,' she murmured.

He smiled a slow, seductive smile that sent her heart rate rocketing. 'In that case…' He unfastened the catch on her jeans. 'Let's see if we can get these jeans to misbehave…'

Satisfied, replete, her body aching in the most pleasurable of ways, Andie drowsed in his arms as Dominic slept. But she couldn't let herself sleep.

If she'd been a different kind of person she would have stayed there. Perhaps convinced Dominic to shower with her when they woke. She would enjoy soaping down that powerful body. Heaven knew what kind of fun they could have with the powerful jets of water in his spacious double shower. Then they could retire to spend the rest of the evening in that enormous bed of his.

But Andie was not that person. There was the

Christmas Eve party she had committed to this evening. As the party planner, she was obliged to call in to see all was well. She also had to check the big tree had made its way there safely—though the eighteen-year-old daughter had texted Andie to thank her, thrilled with the 'real tree'.

There was nothing like the smell of pine resin and the beauty of a natural tree. As eleven-year-old Dominic had known. Her heart went out to that little boy who lived in the damaged soul of the big male, sleeping naked next to her, his arm thrown possessively over her. She was also naked, except for her engagement ring, shining with false promise under the lamplight.

She had agreed to see her family tonight. Tomorrow, Christmas Day, would be the first Christmas lunch she had not spent with them. She was surprised her father had taken it so lightly. 'You have to stand by Dominic, love. That party is not just a job for you now. You're his future wife.'

If only.

Reluctantly, she slid away from Dominic, then quietly got dressed. She would see him in the morning. Tomorrow was Christmas Day, a holiday she loved and he hated. Now she could see why. She ached to turn things around for him—if he would let her.

She looked at his face, more relaxed than she had seen it, and smiled a smile that was bittersweet. They had made love and it had been magnificent. But nothing had changed between them. Tomorrow she was facing the biggest party of her career so far. She would be by the side of the man she had fallen in love with, not knowing for how much longer he would be a part of her life.

When the truth was, she wanted Dominic for Christmas. Not just his body—his heart as well.

Somehow, tomorrow she would have to confess to Dominic the truth of how she felt about him. That she wanted to try a relationship for real. She hoped he felt the same. If so, this would be the best Christmas she had ever had. If not... Well, she couldn't bear to think about *if not*.

CHAPTER FIFTEEN

DOMINIC AWOKE ON Christmas morning as he was accustomed to waking on December the twenty-fifth—alone. It was very early, pale sunlight filtering through the blinds. He reached out his hand to the sofa beside him in the vain hope that Andie might still be there, only to find the leather on that side disappointingly cool to the touch. He closed his eyes again and breathed in the scent of her that lingered in the room, on his skin. Then was overtaken by an anguished rush of longing for her that made him double over with gut-wrenching pain.

He remembered her leaving his side, her quiet footsteps around the room, the rustling as she slid on her clothes. Then her leaning towards him, murmuring that she had to go. She had duties, obligations. He'd pulled her back close to him, tried to convince her with his hands, with his mouth why she should stay. But she'd murmured her regret, kissed him with a quick fierce passion, told him he had jet lag to get over. Then she'd gone.

All he'd wanted to say to her still remained unsaid.

Of course she'd gone to the other people in her life who needed her and loved her. The only commitment she'd made to him was based on the falsehoods he'd engendered and coerced her into. She'd played her role to perfection. So well he was uncertain what might be fact and what might be fiction. But surely making love to him with such passion and tenderness had not been play-acting?

He noticed the bourbon bottle on the desk, lid on, barely touched. This would be the first Christmas he could remember that he hadn't tried to obliterate. The first Christmas that he woke to the knowledge that while Andie might not be here now, she soon would be. And that his perfect, empty house would be filled with people. People who had known hardship like he had and whom he was in the position to help by making their Christmas Day memorable.

Not for the first time, he thought of the possibility of opening a branch of the Underground Help Centre here in Sydney, where it was so obviously needed. Profits from the joint venture with Walter could help fund it. He had much to learn from Walter—he could see it was going to end up a friendship as well as a business partnership.

For the first Christmas in a long time he had something to look forward to—and it was all thanks to Andie.

He hauled himself off the sofa and stretched out the cricks in his back. The sofa was not the best place to sleep—though it had proved perfectly fine for energetic lovemaking. He paused, overwhelmed by memories of the night before. *Andie.* Hunger for her threatened to overwhelm him again—and not just for her beautiful, generous body. He prayed to whatever power that had brought her to him to let him keep her in his life. He hoped she would forgive the way he'd behaved—understand why. And know that it would never happen again.

He headed down the stairs and stood in the entrance hall. Not a trace of the tree remained, thank heaven. He breathed in. And none of that awful smell. Andie had been well meaning but misguided about the tree—now she understood.

The ballroom was all set up, with tables and chairs adorned in various combinations of red and white. A large buffet table area stretched along the wall closest to the kitchen. He'd approved the menu with Gemma and knew within hours it would be groaning with a lavish festive feast. The dishes had been chosen with the diverse backgrounds of the guests in mind—some were refugees experiencing their first Christmas in Australia.

He still couldn't have tolerated a tree in the house but he had to admit to a stirring of interest in the celebrations—more interest than he'd had in Christmas since he'd been a child. Andie was clever—children would love all this and adults should also respond to the nostalgia and hope it evoked. Hadn't she said Christmas was about evoking emotion?

Thanks to the tragedy on Christmas Eve all those years ago, thanks to the way his aunt had treated him in the years that followed, the emotions the season had evoked for him had been unhappy in the extreme. Was there a chance now for him to forge new, happy memories with a kind, loving woman who seemed to understand his struggles?

Andie had said he could trust her, but after his display of anger over the Christmas tree last night would she let herself trust *him*?

There was a large Santa Claus figurine in the corner with rows of canvas, sunshine-themed goody bags stacked around it. Of course it should have been a tree—but the Santa worked okay too as a compromise. The sturdy bags could double as beach bags, the ever-practical Andie had pointed out to him. She had thought of everything. There were gifts there for the volunteers too.

The house seemed to hum with a quiet anticipation and he could feel his spirits rise. Christmas Day with Andie in his house must surely be a step up on the ones he'd been forced to endure up until now.

He swung open the doors and headed to his gym for a workout.

* * *

An hour later Andie arrived with the chef and his crew. Dominic had long given her a pass code to get in and out of fortress Vaucluse.

She was wearing working gear of shorts, T-shirt and sneakers. Later she would change into her beautiful new red lace dress and gorgeous shoes—strappy and red with tassels—in time to greet their guests. She took her dress on its hanger and her bag into the downstairs bathroom. As she did, she noticed the doors to the garden were open and someone was in the pool. She went out to investigate.

Of course it was Dominic, his powerful body spearing through the water. No wonder he had such well-developed muscles with vigorous swimming like this. She watched, mesmerised at his rhythmic strokes, the force of his arms and powerful kick propelling him with athletic grace.

She didn't say anything but maybe her shadow cast on the water alerted him to her presence. Maybe he caught sight of her when he turned his head to breathe. He swam to the edge of the pool and effortlessly pulled himself out of the water, muscles rippling. He wasn't even out of breath.

She almost swooned at the sight of him—could a man be more handsome? Memories of the ecstasy they had given each other the night before flashed through her, tightening her nipples and flooding her body with desire.

His wet hair was slick to his head, the morning sunlight refracted off droplets of water that clung to his powerfully developed shoulders and cut chest, his veins stood out on his biceps, pumped from exertion. And then there were the classic six-pack, the long, strong legs. He didn't have a lot of body hair for such a dark man, but what there was seemed to flag his outrageous masculinity.

She wanted him more than ever. Not just for a night. For many nights. Maybe every night for the rest of her life. There was so much she wanted to say to him but, for all the connection and closeness and *certainty* she had felt last night, she didn't know how to say it.

Her engagement ring glinted on her left hand. The deal with Walter was done. Dominic's Scrooge reputation was likely to be squashed after the party today. How much longer would this ring stay on her finger? What, if anything, would be her role in Dominic's life? She wanted to say something about last night, bring up the subject of the future, but she just couldn't. 'Happy Christmas,' she said instead, forcing every bit of enthusiasm she could muster into her voice.

He grabbed a towel from the back of the chair and slung it around his shoulders, towelling off the excess water. 'H… Happy Christmas to you too,' he said, his voice rusty in the way of someone unused to uttering those particular words. She wondered how long since he had actually wished anyone the Season's greetings.

He looked down into her face and she realised by the expression in his eyes that he might be as uncertain as she was.

Hope flared in her heart. 'Dominic, I—'

'Andie, I—'

They both spoke at the same time. They laughed. Tried again.

'About last night,' he said.

'Yes?' she said.

'I wanted to—'

But she didn't hear what he had to say, didn't get a chance to answer because at that moment the chef called from the doors that opened from the ballroom that Gemma and Eliza were there and needed to be buzzed in.

Dominic groaned his frustration at the terminated conversation. Andie echoed his groan.

'Later,' she said as she turned away, knowing that it would be highly unlikely for them to get another private moment together for the next few hours.

Dominic found the amount of noise two hundred people could generate—especially when so many of them were children—quite astounding. He stood on the edge of the party, still at the meet-

and-greet stage, with appetisers and drinks being passed around by waiters dressed as Christmas elves.

Santa Claus, otherwise known as Rob Cratchit, his Director of Marketing, sidled up next to him. 'It's going even better than I expected,' he said through his fake white beard. 'See that woman over there wiping tomato sauce off the little boy's shirt? She's a journalist, volunteering for the day, and one of your most strident Scrooge critics. She actually called you a multi-million-dollar miser. But I think she's already convinced that today is not some kind of cynical publicity stunt.'

'Good,' said Dominic. Strange that the original aim of this party—to curry favour with Walter Burton—seemed to have become lost. Now it was all about giving people who had it tough a heart-warming experience and a good meal. And enjoying it with Andie by his side.

'Good on you for dressing up as Santa Claus,' he said to Rob. Andie had been right—Rob made the perfect Santa and he had the outgoing personality to carry it off.

'Actually, *you're* the Santa Claus. I talked to one nice lady, a single mum, who said her kids would not have got Christmas lunch or a Christmas present this year, unless a charity had helped out. She said this was so much better than charity. You should mingle—a lot of people want to thank you.'

'I'm not the mingling type,' Dominic said. 'I don't need to be thanked. I just signed the cheques. It should be Andie they're thanking; this was all her idea.'

'She's brilliant,' said Rob. 'Smart of you to snap her up so quickly. You're a lucky man.'

'Yes,' said Dominic, not encouraging further conversation. He'd never been happy discussing his personal life with anyone. The thought that— unless he said something to her—this might be the last day he had with Andie in his life was enough to sink him into a decidedly unfestive gloom.

He hadn't been able to keep his eyes off Andie as she flitted around the room, looking her most beautiful in a very stylish dress of form-fitting lace in a dusky shade of Christmas red. It was modest but hugged every curve and showed off her long, gorgeous legs. He tried not to think of how it had felt to have those legs wrapped around him last night...

'Well, mustn't linger,' said Rob. 'I have to be off and do the *ho-ho-ho* thing.'

As Rob made his way back into the throng, Andie rang a bell for attention and asked everyone to move towards the entrance hall. 'Some of the children and their parents are singing carols for us today.' She'd told Dominic a few of the adults were involved in street choirs and had been happy to run through the carols with the kids.

There was a collective gasp from the 'audience' as they saw the children lined up on the stairs, starting from the tiniest to the teenagers with the adults behind. Again Andie had been right— the stairs made the most amazing showcase for a choir. Each of the choir members wore a plain red T-shirt with the word *'choir'* printed in white lower-case letters. It was perfect, gave them an identity without being ostentatious.

Andie met his gaze from across the room and she smiled. He gave her a discreet thumbs-up. Professional pride? Or something more personal?

The choir started off with the Australian Christmas carol 'Six White Boomers' where Santa's reindeer were replaced by big white kangaroos for the Australian toy delivery. It was a good icebreaker, and had everyone laughing and clapping and singing along with the chorus.

As Dominic watched, he was surprised to see Andie playing guitar up on the balcony with two other guitarists. She was singing too, in a lovely warm soprano. He remembered that photo of her playing guitar in the hallway of her parents' home and realised how much there was he still didn't know about her—and how much he wanted to know.

When the choir switched to classics like 'Silent

Night' and 'Away in a Manger', Dominic found himself transported back to the happy last Christmas when his parents were alive and they'd gone carol singing in their village. *How could he have forgotten?*

The music and the pure young voices resonated and seemed to unlock a well of feeling he'd suppressed—unable perhaps to deal with the pain of it during those years of abuse by his aunt. He'd thought himself incapable of love—because he had been without love. But he *had* been loved back then, by his parents and his grandparents—loved deeply and unconditionally.

He'd yearned for that love again but had never found it. His aunt had done her best to destroy him emotionally but the love that had nurtured him as a young child must have protected him. The realisation struck him—he had loved women incapable of loving him back, and all this time had thought the fault was his when those relationships had failed.

Andie's voice soared above the rest of the choir. Andie, who he sensed had a vast reserve of love locked away since she'd lost her boyfriend. He wanted that love for himself and he wanted to give her the love she needed. How could he tell her that?

He tried to join in with the words of the carol but his throat closed over. He pretended to cough.

Before he made an idiot of himself by breaking down, he pushed his way politely through the crowd and made his way out to the cabana, the only place where he could be alone and gather his thoughts.

But he wasn't alone for long. Andie, her eyes warm with concern, was soon with him. 'Dominic, are you okay?' she said, her hand on his arm. 'I know how you feel about Christmas and I was worried—'

'I'm absolutely fine—better than I've been for a long time,' he said.

He picked up her left hand. 'Take off your ring and give it to me, please.'

Andie froze. She stared at him for a long moment, trying to conceal the pain from the shaft of hurt that had stabbed her heart. So it had come to this so soon. Her use was over. Fake fiancée no longer required. Party planner no longer required. Friend, lover, confidante and whatever else she'd been to him no longer required. *She was surplus to requirements.*

Dominic had proved himself to be generous and thoughtful way beyond her initial expectations of Scrooge. But she must not forget the cold, hard fact—people who got to be billionaires in their twenties must have a ruthless streak. And he'd reneged on his offer that she could keep the ring—

not that she'd had any intention of doing so. To say she was disappointed would be the world's biggest understatement.

She felt as though all the energy and joy was flowing out of her to leave just a husk. The colour drained from her face—she must look like a ghost.

With trembling fingers, she slid off the magnificent ring and gave it back to him, pressing it firmly into the palm of his hand. Her finger felt immediately empty, her hand unbalanced.

'It's yours,' she said and turned on her heel, trying not to stagger. She would not cry. She would not say anything snarky to him. She would just walk out of here with dignity. *This was her worst Christmas Day ever.*

'Wait! Andie! Where are you going?'

She turned back to see Dominic with a look of bewilderment on his handsome, tough face. 'You're not going to leave me here with your ring?'

Now it was her turn to feel bewildered. '*My* ring? Then why—?' she managed to choke out.

He took her hand again and held it in a tight grip. 'I'm not doing a good job of this, am I?'

He drew her closer, cleared his throat. 'Andie, I… I love you, and I'm attempting to ask you to marry me. I'm hoping you'll say "yes", so I can put your ring back on your wedding finger where it belongs, as your *real* fiancé, as a *real* engagement ring. Just like you told me you wanted.'

She was stunned speechless. The colour rushed back into her face.

'Well?' he prompted. 'Andrea Jane Newman, will you do me the honour of becoming my wife?'

Finally she found her words. Although she only needed the one. 'Yes,' she said. 'I say "yes".'

With no further ado, he slid the beautiful ring back into its rightful place. To her happy eyes it seemed to flash even more brilliantly.

'Dominic, I love you too. I think maybe it *was* love at first sight the day I met you. I never really had to lie about that.'

She wound her arms around his neck and kissed him. They kissed for a long time. Until they were interrupted by a loud knock on the door of the pool house. Gemma.

'Hey, you two, I don't know what's going on in there and I don't particularly want to know, but we're about to serve lunch and your presence is required.'

'Oh, yes, of course—we're coming straight away,' Andie called, flustered.

Dominic held her by the arm. 'Not so fast. There's something else I want to ask you. What would you like for Christmas?'

His question threw her. She had to think very hard. But then it came to her. 'All I want for Christmas is for us to get married as soon as possible. I... I don't want to wait. You...you know why.'

Anthony would have wanted this for her—to grab her second chance of happiness. She knew that as certainly as if he'd been there to give her his blessing.

'That suits me fine,' Dominic said. 'The sooner you're my wife the better.'

'Of course it takes a while to organise a wedding. Next month. The month after. I don't want anything too fussy anyway, just simple and private.'

'We'll have to talk to the Party Queens,' he said.

She laughed. 'Great idea. I have a feeling we'll be the best people for the job.'

She could hardly believe this was true, but the look in his eyes told her she could believe it. She wound her arms around his neck again. 'Dominic Hugo Hunt, you've just made this the very best Christmas of my life.'

He heaved a great sigh and she could see it was as if the weight of all those miserable Christmases he'd endured in the past had been thrown off. 'Me too,' he said. 'And all because of you, my wonderful wife-to-be.'

CHAPTER SIXTEEN

ANDIE FOUND HERSELF singing 'Rudolph the Red-Nosed Reindeer' as she drove to Dominic's house five days later. She couldn't remember when she'd last sung in the car—and certainly not such a cheesy carol as 'Rudolph'. No, wait. 'Six White Boomers' was even cheesier. But the choir had been so wonderful at Dominic's Christmas party she'd felt it had become the heart of the very successful party. The carols had stayed in her head.

It had only been significant to her, but it was the first time she'd played her guitar and sung in public since Anthony had died. She'd healed in every way from the trauma of his loss, although she would never forget him. Her future was with Dominic. How could she ever have thought he was not her type?

She didn't think Dominic would be burdened with the Scrooge label for too much longer. One of his most relentless critics had served as a volunteer at the party—and had completely changed her tune. Andie had committed to heart the journalist's article in one of the major newspapers.

Dominic Hunt appears more Santa Claus than Scrooge, having hosted a lavish Christmas party, not for celebrities and wealthy silvertails but for ordinary folk down on their luck. A publicity stunt? No way.

She suspected Dominic's other private philanthropic work would eventually be discovered—probably by the digging of this same journalist. But, with the support of her love and the encouragement of Walter Burton, she thought he was in a better place to handle the revelations of his past if and when they came to light.

Dominic had invited her for a special dinner at his house this evening, though they'd had dinner together every evening since Christmas—and breakfast. She hadn't been here for the last few days; rather, he'd stayed at her place. She didn't want to move in with him until they were married.

But he'd said they had to do something special this evening as they wouldn't be able to spend New Year's Eve together—December the thirty-first would be the Party Queens' busiest night yet.

She was looking forward to dinner together, just the two of them. It was a warm evening and she wore a simple aqua dress that was both cool and elegant. Even though they were now engaged for real, they were still getting to know each other—there was a new discovery each time they got the chance to truly talk.

As she climbed the stairs to his house, she heard the sounds of a classical string quartet playing through the sound system he had piped through the house. Dominic had good taste in music, thank heaven. But when she pushed open the door, she was astounded to see a live quartet playing in the same space where the ill-fated Christmas tree had stood. She smiled her delight. It took some getting used to the extravagant gestures of a billionaire.

Dominic was there to greet her, looking darkly handsome in a tuxedo. She looked down at her simple dress in dismay. 'I didn't realise it was such an occasion or I would have worn something dressier,' she said.

Dominic smiled. 'You look absolutely beautiful. Anyway, if all goes well, you'll be changing into something quite different.'

She tilted her head to the side. 'This is all very intriguing,' she said. 'I'm not quite sure where you're going with it.'

'First of all, I want to say that everything can be cancelled if you don't want to go ahead with it. No pressure.'

For the first time she saw Dominic look like he must have looked as a little boy. He seethed with suppressed excitement and the agony of holding on to a secret he was desperate to share.

'Do tell,' she said, tucking her arm through the crook of his elbow, loving him more in that moment than she had ever loved him.

A big grin split his face. 'I'm going to put my hands over your eyes and lead you into the ball-room.'

'Okay,' she said, bemused. Then she guessed it. The family had been determined to give her an engagement party. Now that she and Dominic actually were genuinely engaged she would happily go along with it. She would act suitably surprised. And be very happy. Getting engaged to this wonderful man was worth celebrating.

She could tell she was at the entrance to the ballroom. 'You can open your eyes now,' said Dominic, removing his hands.

There was a huge cry of 'Surprise!' Andie was astounded to see the happy, smiling faces of all her family and friends as well as a bunch of people she didn't recognise but who were also smiling.

What was more, the ballroom had been transformed. It was exquisitely decorated in shades of white with hints of pale blue. Round tables were set up, dressed with white ruffled cloths and the backs of the chairs looped with antique lace and white roses. It was as if she'd walked into a dream.

She blinked. But it was all still there when she opened her eyes.

Dominic held her close. 'We—your family, your friends, me—have organised a surprise wedding for you.'

Andie had to put her hand to her heart to stop it from pounding out of her chest. 'A wedding!'

She looked further through the open glass doors to see a bridal arch draped with filmy white fabric and white flowers set up among the rows of blue agapanthus blooming in the garden. Again she blinked. Again it was still there when she opened her eyes.

'Your wedding,' said Dominic. '*Our* wedding. You asked to be married as soon as possible. I organised it. With some help from the Party Queens. Actually, a *lot* of help from the Party Queens. Jake Marlow and some other friends of mine are also here.'

'It…it's unbelievable.'

'Only if it's what you want, Andie,' Dominic said, turning to her so just she could hear. 'If it's too much, if you'd rather organise your own wedding in your own time, this can just turn into a celebration of our engagement.'

'No! I want it. It's perfect.' She turned to the expectant people who seemed to have all held their breath in anticipation of her response and gone silent. 'Thank you. I say I do—well, I'm *soon* going to say I do!'

There was an eruption of cheers and happy relieved laughter. 'Here comes the bride,' called out one of her brothers.

Andie felt a swell of joy and happy disbelief. It was usually her organising all the surprise parties. To have Dominic do this for her—well, she felt as if she was falling in love with him all over again.

But the party planner in her couldn't resist checking on the details. 'The rings?' she asked Dominic. He patted his breast pocket. 'Both ready-to-wear couture pieces,' he said.

'And this is all legal?'

'Strictly speaking, you need a month's notice of intent to be married—and we filled out our form less than a month ago. But I got a magistrate to approve a shorter notice period. It's legal all right.'

Her eyes smarted with tears of joy. This was really happening. She was getting married today to the man she adored and in front of the people she loved most in the world.

Her fashion editor friend, Karen, dashed out from the guests and took her by the arm. 'Hey! No tears. I've got my favourite hair and make-up artist on hand and we don't want red eyes and blotchy cheeks. Let's get your make-up done. She's already done your bridesmaids.'

'My bridesmaids?'

'Your sisters, Hannah and Bea, Gemma, Eliza and your little niece, Caitlin. The little nephews are ring-bearers.'

'You guys have thought of everything.'

Turning around to survey the room again, she noticed a fabulous four-tiered wedding cake, covered in creamy frosting and blue sugar forget-me-nots. It was exactly the cake she'd talked about with Gemma. She'd bet it was chocolate cake on the bottom layers and vanilla on the top—Gemma knew she disliked the heavy fruitcake of traditional wedding cakes.

'Wait until you see your wedding dresses,' said Karen.

'Dresses?'

'I've got you a choice of three. You'll love them all but there's one I think you'll choose. It's heavy ivory lace over silk, vintage inspired, covered at the front but swooping to the back.'

'And a veil? I always wanted to wear a veil on my wedding day.' This all felt surreal.

'I've got the most beautiful wisp of silk tulle edged with antique lace. You attach it at the back of a simple halo band twisted with lace and trimmed with pearls. A touch vintage, a touch boho—very Andie. Oh, and your mother's pearl necklace for your "something borrowed".'

'It sounds divine.' She hugged Karen and

thanked her. 'I think you know my taste better than I do myself.'

It *was* divine. The dress, the veil, the silk-covered shoes that tied with ribbons around her ankles, the posy of white old-fashioned roses tied with mingled white and blue ribbon. The bridesmaids in their pale blue vintage style dresses with white rosebuds twisted through their hair. The little boys in adorable mini white tuxedos.

As she walked down the magnificent staircase on her father's arm, Andie didn't need the guests' *oohs* and *aahs* to know she looked her best and the bridal party was breathtaking. She felt surrounded by the people she cared for most—and who cared for her. She wouldn't wish anything to be different.

Dominic was waiting for her at the wedding arch, flanked by his best man, Jake Marlow—tall, broad-shouldered, blond and not at all the geek she'd imagined him to be—with her brothers and Rob Cratchit as groomsmen.

She knew she had to walk a stately, graceful bride's walk towards her husband-to-be. But she had to resist the temptation to pick up her skirts and run to him and the start of their new life as husband and wife.

Dominic knew the bridesmaids looked lovely and the little attendants adorable. But he only had eyes for Andie as she walked towards him, her love for him shining from her eyes.

As she neared where he waited for her with the celebrant, a stray breeze picked up the fine layers of her gown's skirts and whirled them up and over her knees. She laughed and made no attempt to pin them down.

As her skirts settled back into place, their glances met and her lips curved in an intimate exchange of a private joke that had meaning only for two. It was just one of many private connections he knew they would share, bonding and strengthening their life as partners in the years of happy marriage that stretched out ahead of them.

Finally she reached him and looked up to him with her dazzling smile. He enfolded her hand in his as he waited with her by his side to give his wholehearted assent to the celebrant's question. 'Do you, Dominic Hugo Hunt, take this woman, Andrea Jane Newman, to be your lawful wedded wife?'

CHAPTER SEVENTEEN

Christmas Day the following year.

ANDIE STOOD WITHIN the protective curve of her husband's arm as she admired the fabulous Christmas tree that stood in the entrance of their Vaucluse home. It soared almost to the ceiling and was covered in exquisite ornaments that were set to be the start of their family collection, to be brought out year after year. Brightly wrapped gifts were piled around its base.

Christmas lunch was again being held here today, but this time it was a party for just Andie's family and a few other waifs and strays who appreciated being invited to share their family's celebration.

The big Scrooge-busting party had been such a success that Dominic had committed to holding it every year. But not here this time. This year he'd hired a bigger house with a bigger pool and invited more people. He'd be calling in to greet his guests later in the day.

Andie hadn't had to do a thing for either party. She'd had her input—how could a Party Queen not? But for this private party the decorating, table settings and gift-wrapping had all been done by Dominic and her family.

After much cajoling, Andie had convinced her father to transfer his centre of cooking operations to Dominic's gourmet kitchen—just for this year. Although Dad had grumbled and complained about being away from familiar territory, Andie knew he was secretly delighted at the top-of-the-range equipment in the kitchen. The aromas that were wafting to her from the kitchen certainly smelled like the familiar traditional family favourites her father cooked each year. She couldn't imagine they would taste any less delicious than they would cooked in her parents' kitchen.

It was people who made the joy of Christmas and all the people she cherished the most were here to celebrate with her.

And one more.

The reason for all the disruption lay cradled in her arms. Hugo Andrew Hunt had been born in the early hours of Christmas Eve.

The birth had been straightforward and he was a healthy, strong baby. Andie had insisted on leaving the hospital today to be home for Christmas. Dominic had driven her and Hugo home so slowly and carefully they'd had a line of impatient cars honking their horns behind them by the time they'd got back to Vaucluse. He was over the moon about becoming a father. This was going to be one very loved little boy.

'Weren't you clever, to have our son born on Christmas Eve?' he said.

'I'm good at planning, but not *that* good,' she said. 'He came when he was ready. Maybe... maybe your parents sent him.' She turned her head so she could look up into Dominic's eyes. 'Now Christmas Eve will be a cause for celebration, not mourning, for you.'

'Yes,' he said. 'It will—because of you.'

Andie looked down at the perfect little face of her slumbering son and felt again the rush of fierce love for this precious being she'd felt when the midwife had first laid him on her tummy. He had his father's black hair but it was too soon to tell what colour his eyes would be.

Her husband, he-who-would-never-be-called-Scrooge-again, gently traced the line of little Hugo's cheek with his finger. 'Do you remember how I said last year was the very best Christmas of my life? Scratch that. This one is even better.'

'And they will get better and better,' she promised, turning her head for his kiss.

As they kissed, she heard footsteps on the marble floor and then an excited cry from her sister Bea. 'They're home! Andie, Dominic and baby Hugo are home!'

* * * * *

LARGER-PRINT BOOKS!
GET 2 FREE LARGER-PRINT NOVELS PLUS
2 FREE GIFTS!

♥ HARLEQUIN®

Romance

From the Heart, For the Heart

HRLP15

"All those years ago, why did you push me away? Have
you never wondered what would have happened if you
hadn't?"

"It's never crossed my mind." But his eyes shifted to
her mouth as he spoke.

He's lying. Her throat dried as she realized what that
meant.

He *had* thought about it. And that changed everything.
Almost unconsciously she licked her lips; his throat
tightened as he watched the tip of her tongue slip up to her
top lip and, at the gesture, her heart began to beat faster.

Emboldened, Flora carried on, her voice low and
persuasive. "All those nights we stayed up talking till
dawn. When we visited each other at uni we slept in the
same bed, for goodness' sake. The tents we've shared...
Have you never wondered, not even once? What it would
be like? What *we'd* be like?"

"I…" His eyes were on hers, intent, a heat she had never seen before beginning to burn bright, melting her. "Maybe once or twice." His voice was hoarse. "But we're not like that, Flora. We're more than that."

Flora was dimly aware that there was something important in his words, something fundamental that she should understand, but she didn't want to stop, not now as the heat in his eyes intensified, his gaze locking on hers. If she pushed it now, he would follow. She knew it; she knew it as she knew him.

She also knew that whatever happened, the consequences would be immense. There would be repercussions. Last time they had pretended it had never happened. It was unlikely that would happen again; their friendship would be altered forever. Could she live with that?

Could she live without trying? Laugh it off as lack of sleep and too much schnapps? Now that she had come so far…

No, not when he was looking at her like that. Heat and questions and desire mingling in his eyes, just as she had always dreamed. *I want you to go for what you want.* That was what he'd told her.

She wanted him.

"Kiss me, Alex," she said softly.

And before he could reply or pull away, Flora stepped in, put her hand on his shoulder and, raising herself on her tiptoes, she pressed her mouth to his.

Don't miss
PROPOSAL AT THE WINTER BALL by Jessica Gilmore,
available December 2015 wherever
Harlequin® Romance books and ebooks are sold.

www.Harlequin.com

HREXP1115